FOREVER CHRISTMAS

FOREVER CHRISTMAS

ROBERT TATE MILLER

THOMAS NELSON
Since 1798

NASHVILLE   MEXICO CITY   RIO DE JANEIRO

Published in Nashville, Tennessee, by Thomas Nelson. Thomas Nelson is a registered trademark of HarperCollins Christian Publishing, Inc.

Thomas Nelson, Inc., titles may be purchased in bulk for educational, business, fund-raising, or sales promotional use. For information, please e-mail SpecialMarkets@ThomasNelson.com.

Cover Design: Connie Gabbert
Cover Photography: Shutterstock

Library of Congress Cataloging-in-Publication Data

Miller, Robert Tate.
  Forever Christmas / Robert Tate Miller.
     pages cm
  ISBN 978-1-4016-9063-2 (hardback)
  1. Married people--Fiction. 2. Wives--Death--Fiction. 3. Bereavement--Fiction. 4. Angels--Fiction. I. Title.
  PS3613.I5526F67 2014
  813'.6--dc23

                          2014015397

Printed in the United States of America
14 15 16 17 18 19 RRD 6 5 4 3 2 1

For Chloe June—the greatest gift of my life.

PROLOGUE

*M*ost kids love Christmas. But for me, it was always a big disappointment.

I can still see myself in my pajamas, sitting beneath the Christmas tree, frantically tearing away Santa Claus wrapping paper. I had to get into that next box for my first peek at the newest and greatest gizmo or gadget, the gift I swore up and down would make me eternally happy.

And if the present I longed for wasn't inside the box, I'd feel let down. Maybe even pout a little. If I did get what I wanted, I usually ended up playing with it for a few days, then losing interest and shoving it into the back of my closet.

Soon my hopes and dreams would shift to the next big thing, the one that looked oh so cool in the commercials. Yet somehow that too always fell short of my expectations.

No matter how many Christmas gifts I received, I was never satisfied. I kept looking, peering around the back of the tree, hoping to find a package that I'd missed. One more present with my name on the tag.

As years went by, this endless cycle of acquisition and

dissatisfaction became a recurring theme in my life. The more I had, the less I appreciated. Life itself became a second-rate toy thrust to the back of the closet, gathering dust.

Ingratitude became my defining characteristic.

Then along came a snowstorm . . . and a Christmas that changed everything.

CHAPTER ONE

*A*ndrew was late again. As Beth meandered through rows of pine trees at Ray's Christmas Tree Lot, she resisted the urge to call her consistently late husband. What good would it do? He'd just apologize as usual, pluck an excuse from the catalog of excuses he kept tucked away in his coat pocket. "Pick out a tree," he'd say. "And I'm sure I'll love it."

Beth sighed, glanced at the time on her iPhone. Two minutes later than the last time she checked.

Ray, the lot owner, tugged at the collar of his plaid shirt as he approached. "So what'll it be, miss?"

"I'll take that one," Beth said. She pointed to a scraggly, glorified twig that looked a bit like Charlie Brown's pathetic tree in *A Charlie Brown Christmas.*

"Really?" Ray stared at her. "He's a scrawny little orphan." Apparently he'd forgotten all the lessons he learned in Salesmanship 101.

"I like underdogs," Beth said. "How much?"

Ray scratched his chin. "Let's see, for a nice lady like you, I can let him go for thirty-five."

"Twenty-five," Beth countered. "And you throw in a stand."

Ray pondered her offer for a beat, then caved. "Deal."

Beth was covered in pine needles by the time she dragged the little tree three blocks from the tree lot at 86th and Park to the Carnegie Hill apartment she shared with her husband. She'd managed to lose a branch or two along the way and wondered if this miserable little pine wouldn't be better off left at the curb for the trash collector.

She paused on the sidewalk and looked up at her apartment window. Dark. Well, at least Andrew hadn't come home and forgotten about her. She rested the tree by the entry door and checked her phone in case she'd missed a text. Nothing.

"Beth, there you are!"

Beth turned to see her husband, Andrew, jogging across the street, his leather carrying case slung over his shoulder, Bluetooth welded to his head.

"There you are!" Beth made no attempt to disguise her annoyance. Andrew held up his index finger, his signal for "I'm on the phone." Beth folded her arms and glared at him as he finished up a business call.

"Al, just call Kimberly, and she'll make the travel arrangements. Okay, gotta run." Andrew clicked off his phone. "Alistair Whitman," he said. He planted a hurried kiss on Beth's cheek. But if he thought dropping the name of his most famous literary client would get him out of his wife's doghouse, he had another thing coming.

4

"Andrew, where were you? I waited at the tree lot for almost an hour."

"Honey, I'm so sorry. The end of the year is crunch time for a literary agent. All my deals are closing. I'm swamped."

"How much effort does it take to send a simple text?" Beth said.

"Beth, I know. I have no excuse." Andrew appraised the tree. "Wow. *That's* our tree?"

Beth glared at him. "Don't you dare, Andrew Farmer. You forfeited the right to be critical."

Andrew smiled and picked up the tree. "I know the perfect spot for it." Beth opened the apartment building entry door, and Andrew plunged through, cracking a branch on the way in.

"Andrew! Careful! Don't hurt him."

"Oh, so it's a *him*, eh?" Andrew tried to tease Beth into a better mood as he fought his way up the narrow stairwell. "I thought trees were supposed to be female."

"You didn't think any such thing."

Andrew was halfway up the stairwell when Lulu, the yippy beast in 4B, bolted from the landing down the steps and through his legs, nearly toppling him over the railing.

Andrew called out as he regained his balance. "Beth! That little mutt Whatshisname's out again!"

"It's Lulu," Beth said. She scooped the little dog up in her arms. "She's not a mutt. She's a West Highland terrier. And it's Whats *her* name."

An old lady's voice hollered down from the second level, "Luluuuu!"

"I've got her, Mrs. Applebee," Beth called back. She pointed her finger at the dog. "You've got to stop sneaking out like that."

Mrs. Applebee stepped out of her apartment and smiled when she saw Beth cradling her Lulu. "Oh, thank you, Beth. What would I do without you?" Beth lifted the squirming dog into the woman's arms. "Would you like to come in for some hot cocoa and Christmas cookies?" Mrs. Applebee said.

"I'd love to, Mrs. A, but Andrew and I are just about to trim our tree." Mrs. Applebee considered Andrew as if noticing him—and the tree—for the first time.

"Oh, your husband's home. Miracles never cease. Well, some other time then. Bye now, and merry Christmas."

"Merry Christmas," Beth said. Mrs. Applebee shot Andrew a disapproving look and vanished inside her apartment.

"That woman hates me," Andrew said.

"She thinks you don't deserve me," Beth said. "She might be right."

Andrew positioned the little tree in the corner by the window. "At least *he* doesn't take up much space."

Beth looked over and smiled. "A little more centered, please."

Andrew shifted the tree six inches to the left. "There. Perfect," Beth said. "How does grilled cheese and tomato soup sound?"

"Fine," Andrew said.

"You know, it's supposed to snow Christmas Eve," Beth said. "I'd love a white Christmas."

"Yeah," Andrew said.

"I have a wonderful idea!" Beth said. "After we decorate the tree, let's light a fire and watch the movie."

"What movie?" Andrew said. He plucked a pine needle from his neck.

"Well, *White Christmas*, of course." Beth sang a few bars of one of the songs from the musical:

> *If you're worried and you can't sleep,*
> *Just count your blessings instead of sheep,*
> *And you'll fall asleep*
> *Counting your blessings.*

Her voice was sweet and perfectly pitched, and Andrew couldn't help but smile. He always loved to hear Beth sing. Then a guilty knot tightened in his gut. She wasn't going to like what he was about to say.

"You know, that sounds great," Andrew said. "But you think we could take a rain check? Or rather a *snow* check. Huh? See what I did with the whole snow theme?" Andrew chuckled at his lame attempt at humor. Beth wasn't smiling. "You're right. Not funny," he said.

"What is it, Andrew? Another business dinner? Because I thought we were going to spend Christmas together."

"Beth, we are. It's not Christmas . . . yet. It's December 22. We have three more days until Christmas."

Beth glared at him and then gave him her back. Andrew knew this wasn't a good sign. Anger was bad, the cold shoulder far worse.

He stopped messing with the tree and walked over to the kitchen counter where she was dumping soup into a pan. Might as well just throw all the cards on the table.

"I have to go to Chicago for a couple days," he said. "But don't worry, I'll be back in plenty of time for Christmas."

Beth paused for a moment to let the news sink in. She then resumed stirring the soup and refused to meet his eye.

"When?" she said.

Andrew knew that disappointed voice all too well.

"Tonight."

CHAPTER TWO

*H*alf an hour later, Andrew stood on the sidewalk next to an idling yellow cab. As the driver hurled his roller bag into the trunk, Andrew looked up at his apartment window. He could see Beth by the tree, tossing on strands of popcorn. "Look at me," he whispered.

He was sure she felt his eyes on her, but she wouldn't turn his way.

"Bud, if you got a six-thirty flight, we'd better hustle," the driver said. Andrew took one last look at Beth and climbed into the backseat of the cab.

When Andrew arrived at first-class seat 3B on his flight to Chicago, he found a twentysomething beauty occupying 3A. She flashed him a sexy smile as he stashed his carry-on bag in the overhead compartment. It was bad enough leaving his wife on Christmas weekend, but if Beth knew his assistant, Kimberly, was along on this junket, he'd have hell to pay.

When Andrew hired Columbia graduate Kimberly Garner the previous summer, he had no idea it would spell trouble for his marriage. He was impressed with Kimberly from the moment he met her. She was sharp, funny, and ambitious, and he sensed she would soon be moving up the agency ladder. However, when he introduced her to Beth at a company party, he picked up an immediate friction between them. Kimberly poured on the charm in an attempt to win over her boss's spouse, but Beth was reserved, not her usual friendly self.

"She's very pretty," Beth said on the cab ride home that night. "And she has an eye for you." Andrew laughed, told her she was wrong, that Kimberly looked on him as a mentor. But Beth wasn't convinced. From then on, if she had to speak to Kimberly on the phone, Beth was short and to the point. When Kimberly's name came up, she would noticeably tense up.

"Beth, I have lots of assistants. Kimberly's one of many. And she has a boyfriend."

In reality, Kimberly had broken off with the guy she'd been dating a few weeks after coming to work for Andrew's agency. A fact he neglected to mention.

Even though he went out of his way to diminish Kimberly's role in his work life, she remained a touchy subject. And the truth was, Beth's suspicions were warranted. It quickly became obvious that Andrew's beautiful protégé had designs on him. He'd be a fool not to notice the way Kimberly looked at him, how she playfully fine-tuned his hair or adjusted his tie when he was about to head into a meeting. Her flirtations stroked his male ego, but in order to assuage his guilt, Andrew convinced himself it was nothing more than a harmless office crush.

Still, he sensed the day of reckoning was coming, and sooner rather than later. How would he react, he wondered, if Kimberly decided to act on her infatuation?

And that was all the more reason to keep Kimberly's presence on the Chicago trip on the down low. What your wife doesn't know can't get you into trouble.

"Hey, handsome," Kimberly said. "Thought you were going to miss the flight." She took a sip of her cocktail and let her glossed lips linger on the rim of the glass.

Andrew closed the overhead compartment and slipped into the seat beside her. "Almost did. Midtown Tunnel's a parking lot."

Kimberly had already ordered him a Scotch on the rocks and was reading the galley of the novel belonging to the young Chicago writer they were hoping to sign. She thumbed through the pages of the manuscript.

"A bit derivative," she said.

"We're agents," Andrew said. "Our job isn't to smell it but sell it."

"First we have to sign her," Kimberly said.

"It's in the bag," Andrew said. "That's why I make the big bucks."

Back at the apartment, Beth kept occupied with cookie baking, gift wrapping, and last-minute Christmas card writing. She promised herself she'd keep her cool. But when she burned a batch of snowman sugar cookies, she angrily dumped the tray in the garbage can and dropped the pan in the sink with a loud clang.

Why would Andrew leave her like this at the start of the holiday weekend? She felt like calling him and telling him off once and for all.

What had happened to him? To them?

Her eyes drifted to an old, familiar snapshot photo stuck by a fruit-shaped magnet to the refrigerator door. Andrew and Beth posing with Andrew's mother, Emma, at Christmastime, when they were in their early teens. Emma had her arms around them, and though she was smiling, there was sorrow in her eyes.

Growing up together in tiny River Falls, Pennsylvania, Andy Farmer and Beth McCarthy were practically inseparable. They met on a sweltering summer day in a lukewarm kiddie pool in Beth's backyard. Andy was four, Beth three. He was a sweet, sensitive little boy who seemed grown up beyond his years. He wore little sweater vests and bow ties and looked like a miniature Alex P. Keaton. Andy was polite to a fault. It was always "yes, sir" or "yes, ma'am." Adults adored him.

When she reflected back on those early days, Beth could see that young Andrew was forced to be the man around the house long before he was ready. His salesman father, Henry, was on the road most of the time, and the rare times he was home, he preferred to lounge in his easy chair and "catch up on his TV."

Beth could almost hear the ominous words: "Son, I need to speak with you about something."

Andrew had told her every detail about that moment, details

that were burned into his memory. Twelve-year-old Andy was sitting at the little oak desk in his room finishing up his math homework when his mother came in to break the news. It was the third of October, and a cool autumn breeze blew through his open window. As the years went by, Andrew would think back to that moment and marvel at how many minute details he could remember. He could even remember how many times his neighbor's dog barked: six.

"It's about your father," Emma Farmer said.

"What about Dad?" His heart was beating fast. He knew this wasn't going to be good. "Is he okay?"

"He's left us," Emma said. "He's found someone else. Another woman."

That someone else turned out to be a young waitress he'd met on one of his sales trips. Not long after the conversation in Andrew's room, Emma slipped into a deep depression. And try as young Andy might to cheer her up, she never came out of it.

Two years after her husband left her for good, Emma Farmer fell ill one afternoon and died three days later. Andrew was holding one of his mom's hands when she passed; Beth was holding the other.

Andrew didn't even bother to try to contact his dad to give him the news of his wife's passing. He waited until after his mother's funeral and then sent Henry a terse note: *Mom's dead. Just thought you should know.* From that day forward, Andrew wanted nothing more to do with his father.

In the weeks following his mother's death, Andrew tried his best to push Beth away, but she refused to let him. Late one night, in a fit of rage, he called and told her he wanted to meet her by the bandstand in Town Square. Even though it was well past her curfew, Beth could tell her friend was deeply troubled, so she slipped past her sleeping parents and headed for the rendezvous.

When Beth approached the bandstand, she saw Andrew pacing like a caged cat. "Andy, what is it? What's wrong?"

Andrew wheeled on her, and she could see the pain and rage in his eyes.

"I hate him, Beth. You hear me? I HATE him!" he said. "And I need you to hate him too."

"Andrew . . . ?"

"Say it! Say that you hate him as much as I do. If you're really my friend, say it." Beth watched as hot tears rolled down Andrew's face. His voice lowered and he struggled to choke back his sobs. "I need to know. Say you hate him, or we're done."

Beth slowly shook her head. "I'm sorry, Andy. I don't. I can't. And if having to hate your dad is a condition of our friendship, then I'm sorry. I guess we can't be friends anymore."

Andrew stared at her as if he couldn't believe what he was hearing.

"I wish you the best, Andy," Beth said. "I really do. And I'll miss you."

Beth walked away quickly to hide her tears. She wanted to look back at him, to tell him that she loved him, but she knew that would be the wrong thing to do. She knew how much he was hurting, and she knew that she couldn't help him until he was ready to help himself.

They didn't speak for two months. Then one rainy school

morning Andrew was waiting for Beth when she came out of her house. He held an umbrella for her on the five-block walk to River Falls High while he let himself get soaked to the bone. That was Andrew's way of saying he was sorry. He never mentioned their quarrel.

Beth was happy to have her friend back, but she worried about her Andy, about the rage and grief he kept bottled up inside. He hated Henry Farmer for his betrayal, for not being there, and there was no talking him out of it.

And she knew that someday the emotional bill would come due.

CHAPTER THREE

*B*eth could still hear her mother's voice: "Beth, if you know what's good for you, you'll marry that boy. He's a keeper." Beth was only six when her mom began the campaign, but she took it to heart anyway. It just made sense. Andy Farmer was a nice boy, he was her best friend, and he was pretty darn cute to boot.

By the time the childhood sweethearts reached their senior year at River Falls High, Andy and Beth had become best friends, confidants, and soul mates. On graduation night, just after the stroke of midnight, Andrew got down on one knee in the center of Town Square and took Beth's hand.

"I love you, Beth McCarthy. So marry me, and make me the happiest man on earth." While Andrew nervously spoke the words he later told her he'd rehearsed time and again in the bathroom mirror, Beth gazed down at him, happy tears streaming down her face. He slipped his mother's engagement ring on her finger. Beth was so overcome with emotion all she could do was nod up and down.

Beth and Andrew decided that, hard as it might be, they

should defer their wedding plans until after they graduated from college. So, two months after graduation, Andrew headed off to Carnegie Mellon University in Pittsburgh. Valedictorian Beth had received half a dozen scholarships to some of the best schools on the East Coast, but she had a plan. She would stay home and go to night school at River Falls College so she could start her own local charity.

Beth's experience volunteering at a local nursing home during high school opened her eyes to a pressing need. She found that many older people didn't really need to be in the nursing home. They just needed a little help to be able to stay in their homes. They needed a little support, a little company. Beth wanted to give them both, so six months after high school graduation, she founded Best Buddies. The all-volunteer charity performed any number of useful services for seniors. Buddies would read to those who could no longer see so well, prepare and deliver meals for shut-ins, accompany their older buddies on walks, or just pop in for a cup of coffee and a chat.

When the local paper interviewed her about her new enterprise, Beth said, "I just hate the idea of someone feeling alone."

Andrew teased her when he called from college. "Beth McCarthy, enemy of loneliness." But he was proud of her. She was only eighteen and already making a difference.

On June 7, 2002, dozens of family and friends gathered in the chapel on River Falls Town Square to witness the long-awaited wedding of Andrew Gerard Farmer and Elizabeth Anne McCarthy. She was twenty-two, he twenty-three, and both were recent college graduates.

In his wedding toast to his bride, Andrew said, "Beth, I can't even remember life before you. You have always been there for me, and come what may, I promise to always be there for you. As long as I'm around, you will never be alone."

And with a pair of "I dos," their wedded life began.

As they slow danced cheek to cheek to Nat King Cole's "Unforgettable," Beth looked into her new husband's eyes and felt a sudden twinge of sadness.

She wondered if this was as good as it was ever going to get.

"Beth, I want to move to New York."

It was a mere four months after their wedding that the restless Andrew broached the subject. Beth was surprised to find that he already had a ten-year plan all laid out—a plan he hadn't even bothered to run by his new bride. "I talked to one of my old English profs at Carnegie," Andrew said. "He thinks he can get me a job in the mail room of a literary agency."

"You want to be an agent?" Beth said.

"No, I'm going to be a novelist. A famous novelist. The agency's a way for us to make ends meet, and when I'm done with my book, I can slip it to one of the agents at the firm. I'll already have a leg up."

Beth felt her heart sink as she watched her husband's eyes dance with excitement. She had hoped they could build a life there in River Falls, the place she loved most of all. But Andrew had his sights set on a life of adventure. His dreams were far too big for a little town in northwest Pennsylvania. So when he pressed her for an answer, Beth simply smiled and said, "Sounds wonderful."

Late in the spring of 2003, Beth and Andrew Farmer found a new home in an eclectic little neighborhood in New York's East Village. Beth spent her final months in River Falls training a volunteer staff of six to take over Best Buddies. She agreed to stay on as a consultant and would call in twice a week to make sure everything was running smoothly.

Their first apartment was only one room, about the size of a very large closet. It was a far cry from River Falls, but Beth determined she was going to make it work, that she was going to be happy in their new environs. She decided she was going to become a "city girl" come what may.

Beth always looked back fondly on those early years of marriage. Resources were meager, but there was lots of love and fun. They had "date night," "movie night," and "breakfast night," and, for a while anyway, they kept to the schedule faithfully.

While Andrew was off sorting mail and dreaming of bigger things, Beth shuffled from job to job. She worked at a record store, a flower shop, and a grocery. When Hector the flower vendor confided that his eight-year-old daughter, Rosa, was struggling with her schoolwork, Beth offered to tutor her for free.

Beth loved the work, and Hector noticed how quickly Rosa progressed from a C to an A student. He recommended that Beth put her tutoring skills to wider use.

"You should open a tutoring center," the flower vendor said. "Once I tell people what you did for my Rosa, they'll be lining up at your door."

Beth loved tutoring Rosa, loved the satisfaction and fulfillment it gave her, loved especially the "aha moment" when the girl finally understood and her pretty brown eyes would light up.

She loved teaching, but she wanted to do it on her own terms. The more she thought about it, the more she concluded that Hector might be right. The idea of opening her own tutoring center excited her every bit as much as her vision for Best Buddies.

"You'll never make it work," Andrew said. "Why would a parent pay you for something they get for free at public school?"

Beth forced herself to push aside Andrew's doubts and gave it a go. She printed up flyers and spread them throughout the neighborhood. At first, it looked as if Andrew might be right. Nobody responded. Then one day the phone started ringing, and before long, she was tutoring two students, then three, then half a dozen.

Beth held her sessions three afternoons a week in a study room at the public library. She worked with her students on math, history, and English.

Beth's little enterprise was up and running, but at the cost of quality time with her husband. By the time she got home, Andrew had already eaten and would be sprawled out on the couch watching television or reading author submissions for his boss.

Not that he complained; she was doing something she loved, he said, and he wanted her to be happy. And the tutoring income, meager as it was, helped make ends meet.

Still, something told her it was a step in the wrong direction.

If weekdays were busy, at least the weekends were cherished. Every Saturday morning Andrew and Beth rode the subway to 72nd and Central Park West. They'd spend a few hours walking in the park, picnicking, or people watching.

Beth loved those quiet days. They had long talks, dreamed together about the future, about starting a family, about making enough money to flee the city and buy a farmhouse in some Norman Rockwellian Vermont town.

Beth wanted kids more than anything in the world. She couldn't picture the farmhouse without imagining their children running around in the front yard. She was ready to start a family, just like they'd always talked about.

But Andrew wanted to wait. Whenever she brought the subject up, he would always say, "When we're ready. When we're ready." When they celebrated their fifth anniversary still childless, Beth wondered if "ready" would ever arrive.

After three years working in the mail room by day and on his literary masterpiece by night, Andrew was promoted to an agent's assistant. This meant a little more pay, but more importantly, it opened Andrew's eyes to his true career purpose.

"Beth, I no longer want to write novels. I want to sell them. Lots of them."

By this time he'd come to the conclusion that while he was

only an average writer, he had a real knack for what would sell. "Don't smell it, sell it," agency founder Frank Townsend had inscribed on a plaque in his penthouse office. Andrew took that dictum to heart. He soon learned that good writing and salable writing didn't necessarily go hand in hand. As a matter of fact, they were often two very different animals, as Beth could well attest. She sometimes read the author submissions Andrew brought home and turned up her nose.

"Honey, this is terrible. How can you even consider representing this garbage?"

"Don't smell it, sell it," Andrew said. "A novel doesn't have to be good to make a boatload of money."

Andrew's knack for taking hackneyed stories from middling writers and turning out bestsellers quickly made him the new wunderkind at Townsend Literary. He soon leapfrogged more experienced assistants to become a full-fledged agent.

"You have the gift, Farmer," Townsend said to Andrew the morning he kicked him upstairs. "You understand that it's not about prose, it's about perception."

Agency clients loved Andrew and were soon jockeying to have him represent their latest masterpiece. His salary tripled overnight, and he and Beth were able to abandon their cramped Village walk-up for a tiny apartment in the upscale Carnegie Hill neighborhood. They were now just two blocks from Central Park.

Beth was thrilled for her husband's success, but a part of her missed their old East Village neighborhood. She had managed to make it her own and had grown to love every nuance, eccentricity, nook, and cranny. She missed the corner market. She missed

Pedro, the guy she bought a latte from every morning, and Sully, the chatty mail carrier. She missed Hector, the flower guy. They all knew Beth, and she knew all about them. She knew their kids' names and what grade they were in, their birthdays, their hopes and dreams.

Andrew couldn't understand how Beth could miss the dingy, cramped apartment or the low-rent neighborhood. He had been so focused on getting out he hadn't stopped to take a good look around. While everybody on the block knew Beth, nobody knew Andrew Farmer.

"I don't get why you aren't as stoked about the move as I am, Beth," Andrew said. "This is the brass ring. We've arrived!"

Beth didn't know how to tell her husband that her "brass ring" had nothing to do with square footage or real estate value or prestige. She just wanted to live in a neighborhood where people knew and liked each other. She wanted to be a part of a family that extended beyond her own stoop.

Beth had a hard time making friends in Carnegie Hill. Most of the new neighbors seemed too busy or preoccupied to respond to her friendly overtures. The only neighbor who spoke more than two words to her was old Mrs. Applebee, who lived on the same floor a few doors down.

Upward of ninety, Dora Applebee had been a widow for nearly half a century and had lived in the building since the end of World War II. Her dog, Lulu, was her "baby." The spoiled, yappy little Westie loved giving her elderly owner the slip from time to time. She'd take advantage of Mrs. A's forgetfulness and dart out the door and down the stairs. If the dog was lucky, somebody would be coming through the front door, and she could slip out into the wilds of Manhattan for a little romp.

Beth was summoned to fetch the little vagabond on any number of occasions, and Mrs. Applebee loved her for it.

"Beth, you're such a sweet girl. If my grandson wasn't such a schmuck, I'd introduce you."

"That's all right, Mrs. Applebee. I'm already married. Remember?"

Old Mrs. Applebee knew well enough that Beth was married, but she only reluctantly admitted to Andrew's existence. Beth found this humorous; Andrew found it annoying.

"I ordered my steak medium rare, not medium well. You do know the difference, don't you?"

Beth remembered all too vividly how Andrew reprimanded the waiter across a candlelit table at Chianti's, her favorite restaurant in Little Italy. It was her birthday, and Andrew had taken her out for dinner. But instead of having an enjoyable night out, he seemed agitated and tense, and spent most of the evening talking about work and returning phone calls.

She hated to admit it, but this had become the norm. And watching what a little success had done to her husband made Beth long even more for days gone by.

She chalked it up to the pressures of his new job, but it was more than that. Andrew had begun to believe his own notices, the pats on the back and "attaboys" soaking into his psyche.

Most disconcerting, Beth sensed that he believed he was outgrowing her. He often talked down to her or harped about how she couldn't comprehend what his career demanded of him. "Of course, you don't have a *real* job," he said. "So how could you possibly understand?"

Despite what Andrew thought, Beth *did* have a real job. Her tutoring enterprise had grown into a full-fledged educational center. By the time the Farmers moved to Carnegie Hill, the Little Red Schoolhouse Tutoring Center was thriving, catering specifically to children with special needs. She had six employees and rented a cozy storefront on Lexington Avenue with a bright red awning.

In addition, Beth kept in contact with her Best Buddies staff back in River Falls, but she was always careful to avoid mentioning that to Andrew. She had made that mistake once.

"Stop living in the past, Beth," he said. "Most women would kill for your life."

Most women, maybe. But not Beth Farmer. As much as she'd grown to love certain aspects of big-city life, home was still home and never far from her heart. She often wondered what their lives would have been like if they'd settled down in the little town where they grew up. But she knew better than to voice her doubts.

Of one thing she was certain. The dream they'd shared as teenagers had vanished. Their history, their memories, their shared experiences. The future they'd planned together. The two kids—a boy and a girl, Andrew always insisted. "A little you and a little me."

Gone. All of it sucked into the black hole of Andrew's ambition. His precious career. The money. The accolades. The self-absorption.

And now their marriage, too, on shaky ground.

CHAPTER FOUR

By the time his plane touched down at Chicago's O'Hare Airport, Andrew had already had three drinks too many. Kimberly suggested they go straight to dinner to prep for the next day's writer meeting.

They dined at the Chicago Cut Steakhouse and reviewed strategy for wooing the rumored-to-be-headstrong writer Jackie de Wulf. Kimberly asked that she be allowed to soften her up before Andrew swooped in to close the deal. Kimberly watched him closely as she cut into her porterhouse. "So how are things on the home front?"

"Fine," Andrew said. "Why wouldn't they be?"

Kimberly shrugged. "I don't know. You just seem a little distracted."

"Just thinking about the client."

"Oh. Too bad." Kimberly smiled coyly and glanced down at her low-cut neckline. "I was hoping *I* might be the cause of your distraction."

Andrew looked away, at a loss for how to respond.

Kimberly seemed to sense she'd raised his temperature.

"Andrew, just know that . . . if you ever need someone to talk to, I have pretty good ears."

Andrew struggled with an uneasy mixture of flattery and guilt. He shouldn't be having this conversation.

Kimberly smiled warmly, raised her wineglass. "To success."

They touched glasses, and Kimberly's eyes lingered on Andrew until he was forced to look away.

Andrew and Kimberly arrived at the Peninsula Hotel by taxi just after ten and checked in. As they exited the elevator on the seventh floor, Kimberly invited him to her room for a nightcap and to review their strategy for the next day's meeting. "Come on, it's still early."

Andrew yawned. "I'd better take a rain check. I want to be sharp for our meeting."

Kimberly nodded, but he could tell she was disappointed. "All right, then," she said. "If you change your mind, you know my room number."

Andrew watched her head down the hallway toward her room and drew a deep breath. He could no longer deny it: he was teetering on a precarious cliff.

And Kimberly would love to pull him over the edge.

When Andrew got to his room, he checked his cell phone and had a voice mail waiting from Beth.

"Hi, it's me. Just wanted to make sure you got there okay. I'm going to bed, so I'll talk to you tomorrow after your meeting."

Andrew thought about calling and waking her up, then decided against it. She was still mad at him, that much he could tell. But at least she called.

Andrew and Kimberly joined their prospective client for lunch the next day in a booth at Lou Mitchell's on West Jackson Boulevard. Jackie de Wulf was only twenty-seven, but her jaded cynicism made her seem much older. She was brash and shrill and knew everybody in the joint by name, including the homeless guys who lingered outside.

Jackie was not one to mince words and quickly made it apparent she was not the least bit impressed that a hotshot New York literary agent had flown to see her two days before Christmas. She expected no less for a writer with her gifts.

"I don't trust you agent types," she said. "Especially ones that look like you two."

"Oh? How do we look?" Kimberly said.

"He looks like a snake oil salesman, and you look like the snooty girl who blackballed me from the sorority."

Kimberly laughed. "You think I'm the sorority type?"

"You got the face, the bod, the hair. You saying I'm wrong?"

"Dead wrong," Kimberly said. Andrew worried that an epic catfight was about to derail the meeting and their chances of signing the hot, young writer.

"I was in college less than a year," Kimberly said. "And then I was arrested."

"Arrested?" Jackie said. "For what? Too much hairspray?"

Kimberly smiled. "Resisting arrest. It was during a sit-in to protest the Iraq war. I punched a cop who happened to grab me a little too low on my anatomy. I have a pretty good right hook, and he lost a couple of teeth. For some reason, college didn't want me back after that."

Andrew gaped at Kimberly. Something she'd failed to mention in the job interview.

Jackie de Wulf took Kimberly's measure, and for a moment, Andrew wasn't sure which way it was going to turn. Then the writer slowly nodded and looked over at Andrew. "And how'd you come to work for this suit?"

"I work *with* him, not *for* him," Kimberly said. "And don't let the Armani and pretty-boy look fool you. Andrew's a lot like me, not afraid to kick some butt when he has to. You'd be a fool if you didn't sign with him. Sorry to be so blunt."

Jackie sat back, a glimmer of a smile creeping into her eyes. Apparently Kimberly's tough-girl gamble might have paid off.

Andrew raised his wineglass. "To the girl with the killer right hook." It was late evening, and Andrew and Kimberly shared a candlelit table for two back at the Peninsula's Pierrot Gourmet. They clinked glasses of red wine. "I cannot believe you reeled her in with that cockamamie story."

"Who said it was a story?"

Andrew raised his eyebrows. Who was this woman sitting across from him?

"Okay," she said. "I fudged a little bit. But it worked, right?"

Andrew grinned. "Sure did. You're going to make a great agent someday."

"So I guess this means you're happy I came along," Kimberly said.

"Of course." Andrew took a sip of his wine. "I couldn't have signed her without you."

"Is that the only reason?"

"What do you mean?"

Kimberly's voice dropped to a whisper. "I think you know."

Andrew swallowed hard. He had to get out of there. He could almost feel himself clinging to the cliff edge, with his fingers slipping.

"I think I'd better call it a night," he said. He drained his wineglass and slid his chair back from the table.

Kimberly leaned back in her chair and slowly nodded. "Me too," she said.

But her eyes said something else entirely.

An hour later Andrew sat on the edge of his hotel room bed in his pajamas and robe, cell phone in hand. He thought about Kimberly in her room down the hall and felt a wave of relief. He'd done the right thing; he'd dodged a bullet. Tomorrow they'd go back to

New York, and the first day back after the holidays he'd request to have her transferred to another agent. Why tempt fate?

He wanted to call Beth to share the day's good news, but how could he tell her about signing the client without mentioning Kimberly? What would he say? Should he just tell her the truth? She was already mad at him; a confession of his deceitfulness would only make it worse.

He sighed and laid the phone on the nightstand. She was probably already asleep. Maybe he should wait until morning. Then again, he hadn't talked to her all day. She'd be worried.

A knock on the door stirred him from his thoughts. He opened it to find Kimberly standing there, dressed in a Chicago Bears sweatshirt and shorts.

"Kimberly? You're still up?" Andrew said.

"Too excited to sleep." She held up a thick, dog-eared manuscript. "Andrew, I think I've found our next client."

"You brought submission manuscripts with you?"

"A few," she said. "No point in wasting time."

Andrew couldn't help being impressed. Whatever else this woman might be, she was certainly a go-getter. "Okay . . ."

"His name is Calvin Wright—the author, not the character," she said. "He's African American. It's his first novel, and I think he's really, really good. Not just salable—well, that too—but actually *good*." She stepped into the room and launched into an animated summary of the plotline.

Fifteen minutes later, when she had barely taken a breath, Andrew raised a hand to stop her. "Hold on," he said. He went to the minibar and opened the fridge door. "What are you drinking?"

"What do you think of the story?" Kimberly said.

Andrew left her hanging for a moment. "I think it has potential."

Kimberly beamed. "In that case, I'll have a soda water on the rocks." Andrew took out the soda water, plopped it on the counter. He checked the ice bucket. Empty.

"Need to make an ice run. Be right back." Andrew paused before heading out the door. "I really do like it," he said.

As he walked down the carpeted hotel corridor, ice bucket in hand, Andrew imagined Kimberly back in his suite, checking her hair in the mirror. Her motive for showing up in his room was not solely to talk about a potential new client, and they both knew it.

He found the ice machine alcove at the end of the hallway, filled the bucket, then leaned his head on the machine.

Might as well stall his return for as long as possible.

Back in Carnegie Hill, Beth was curled up in a chair by the window, her favorite cozy blanket draped over her, her fingers wrapped around a mug of hot cocoa. Why hadn't Andrew called her all day? The digital clock on the lamp table read 11:23. Next to it sat a framed wedding photo. Not the official one, but an outtake: Beth shoving a piece of wedding cake in Andrew's mouth and missing to the north, smearing his nose. They were both laughing, thoroughly relishing the carefree moment.

Beth took a sip of cocoa and mustered a smile. She had just let him walk out without so much as a kiss good-bye. What if he were in an accident? What if his plane went down? What if she never saw him again, never got the chance to make things right?

Beth picked up her cell phone and stared at it for a moment as if expecting Siri to tell her what to do. She shouldn't have to be the one to reach out. He should be calling her. But Beth had long since come to realize that she was always the one to make the first overture.

She breathed a pained sigh and dialed his number.

"Hello?"

The voice was female, and for a moment, Beth thought she'd dialed the wrong number. But that was impossible. Andrew's cell was programmed into her phone.

Maybe he'd lost his phone somewhere and some stranger had answered, hoping to discover the rightful owner. But no, the voice was familiar. Beth had heard that voice many times before when she'd called him at the office.

Kimberly.

Beth yanked the phone away from her ear and stared at it as she heard the voice repeat, "Hello?" Kimberly had to know it was Andrew's wife calling. She had to be looking at Beth's face, smiling up at her from Andrew's phone.

Beth hung up and tossed the phone away as if it were radioactive. Kimberly knew who it was. She knew, and she didn't care.

Which had to mean that Andrew didn't care either. About Beth, about their life together, about . . .

About anything that mattered.

CHAPTER FIVE

When Andrew finally returned to his suite with the ice, he found Kimberly stretched out on the bed. She smiled at him. "I thought you'd fallen down the elevator shaft or something."

Andrew ignored the remark and took the ice bucket over to the bar counter. He slowly started plunking ice cubes into their glasses. He knew exactly what she was thinking, knew what she wanted. What terrified him most was the recognition that deep in his heart of hearts, he might just want it too.

But he also knew that wanting it was a far cry from acting on it. Giving in to temptation would send his life into a downward spiral that could destroy everything he'd always believed in, everything he'd worked for. He would lose every shred of self-respect. Not to mention the best friend he'd ever had and the one true love of his life.

But there they were, alone in a hotel room. Kimberly was ready and willing and beautiful. Maybe he could have it both ways. Maybe Beth would never find out.

He flinched as Kimberly wrapped her arms around him from behind. He hadn't heard her coming.

"Wow, somebody's sure jumpy tonight," she said.

Andrew put the glasses down, gently removed her arms from his chest, and turned to face her.

"Kimberly, listen . . ."

"Shhh," she said. She put a finger to his lips. "Hear me out, okay? I think you're an amazing man. You're smart and talented and you know exactly where you want to go."

"Kimberly—"

"Wait. I'm not done. Think about it. We are perfect for each other. We're cut from the same cloth; we both want the same things. And, most importantly, I . . . I really care about you, Andrew. I think I might be in love with you."

"Kimberly, please."

"Andrew, I know you're married, so we can take it slow. I promise I won't pressure you." Kimberly put a hand on his face, forced him to meet her gaze.

"I know you want me too. I can feel it." Kimberly moved to kiss him, but Andrew held her off. This had already gone too far. Way too far.

He moved away from her. "Kimberly, I need you to listen to me now. This isn't going to happen. I'm a married man, and I could never—would never—cheat on my wife. I've loved Beth all my life, and that's not about to change."

Kimberly gave him a wounded look, and her eyes welled up with tears. "Oh, so . . . that's it?"

"Yes," Andrew said. "That's it."

She crossed her arms and bit her lip. He couldn't tell if she was angry or hurt—or both. "Please, Kimberly, try to understand.

I think you're a wonderful person. You're smart and kind and beautiful—"

"Spare me, Andrew," she said. "I'm a big girl. I don't need a pep talk. I get it. You're not interested. Sorry to be so presumptuous."

"I hope I haven't led you on . . ."

"Don't worry about it." Kimberly snatched up the manuscript and headed for the door. "It's fine."

"Kimberly, please don't go like this," Andrew said. But he didn't mean it. He wanted her out.

She turned in the doorway, and suddenly the angry home wrecker had vanished. In her place was a little girl with a broken heart. A tear rolled down her cheek. "Beth is one lucky lady," she said. Then she was gone.

CHAPTER SIX

ndrew called Beth the next morning, and it went straight to voice mail. He opted to text her instead. *2:30 flight. Home by 6.* An hour later he checked out of the Peninsula and joined Kimberly in a limo to O'Hare.

Andrew took measure of his assistant's mood. Cordial but cool. She did her best to pretend the previous night never happened and spent most of the ride to the airport on her iPhone. But as they rolled down Michigan Avenue, she casually let a little more leg show than was usual for a December day in Chicago, as if to remind her boss what he'd left on the table.

At the airport, they discovered their two-thirty back to JFK had been delayed indefinitely due to a Christmas snowstorm that had socked the Eastern Seaboard. Kimberly took a seat at the gate as far away from Andrew as possible and lost herself in her iPad. Andrew found an airport bar, ordered a whiskey sour, and tried to get in touch with Beth again. Still no answer.

More than four hours later, the announcement came that Andrew's flight to JFK would soon begin boarding. When he got to his first-class seat, he discovered that Kimberly had switched her seat assignment so that she wouldn't have to sit next to him. Maybe it was for the best. He quickly texted Beth an updated estimated arrival time and settled in for the two-and-a-half-hour flight.

Never mind Kimberly. What he wanted most in the world was to get home to Beth, to make things right, to give her a wonderful Christmas.

A few minutes before 11:00 p.m., Andrew and Kimberly said their terse good-byes at the JFK curb. It was snowing hard, and several inches had already accumulated. Kimberly flagged the first taxi she saw, tossed out a lukewarm "Merry Christmas," and was gone.

"Same to you," Andrew said. As her cab disappeared into the snowstorm, a tremendous sense of relief washed over him. At least that was over. He'd have to face her again after the holidays, but that was more than a week away, and for the time being he could table his worry—at least until after New Year's Day.

He flagged his own taxi and headed home to Beth.

On the way, Andrew had the cab pull to the curb long enough to buy a bouquet of flowers from one of the few markets in Manhattan open late on Christmas Eve. He knew Beth; she'd expect no less after the way he bolted on her so suddenly Friday evening.

As the cab pulled away from his building, Andrew looked up at the apartment window. It was dark inside except for the soft glow from the Christmas tree bulbs. He checked his watch: 11:43 p.m. Beth might already be in bed. He looked at the bouquet, hoped his floral mea culpa would do the trick. He was in no mood for a Christmas Eve confrontation.

As he walked by her apartment, Andrew noticed Mrs. Applebee's door was slightly ajar. He could hear her TV volume turned loud enough to be heard all the way across Central Park.

His own door was unlocked. He pushed it open, stepped into the darkened apartment, and clanked his keys onto the gold tray that sat on the antique table by the door. He peeled off his wool overcoat and scarf and flung them on the rack. The moment he stepped into the dim living room, he saw her: Beth curled up in the easy chair. She was wearing a pullover sweater and jeans, her arms crossed.

"Hey," he said. "Did we forget to pay the Con Ed?"

Beth just stared at him. Andrew knew that look. She was still angry.

"Got your favorite flowers." He held out the bouquet, but Beth made no move to accept them. "Listen . . ." Andrew dropped the flowers on the kitchen table. "I'm sorry I had to run off like that. It's just . . . this writer—"

"*She* answered your phone, Andrew."

His stomach lurched, but he tried to bluff it. "Who?"

"Don't give me that. You know exactly who. Kimberly. I recognized her voice. She answered when I called you last night."

Andrew had a brief flash of anger at Kimberly. Why had she answered his cell phone? Stupid, stupid.

"I . . . told you she was coming along," he said.

"Don't lie, Andrew. I deserve better."

"I'm not lying."

The look on her face told him he'd better not push it. "I guess it slipped my mind," he said. "I didn't think it was important."

"Not important? You know she's after you."

"After me? C'mon, Beth. That's not true. She thinks of me as a mentor—"

"Don't patronize me. I want the truth."

"Beth, I—"

"What was she doing with your phone?"

"I don't know. I guess I left it—"

"Was she in your room?"

Andrew hesitated.

"The truth, Andrew. Just tell me the truth."

"She came along for work. I needed help signing the client."

"So, yes, she *was* in your room. And since when do you need help signing a client?"

Beth was out of her chair. She made a beeline for the front door.

"I'm her boss, Beth. We work together. Nothing happened!"

"Then why didn't you tell me she was going?"

Beth grabbed her coat and scarf from the rack and threw them on. Andrew could see she was struggling to keep from melting down in front of him.

"Beth, stop." Andrew put a hand on Beth's arm.

She jerked away. "Don't touch me! I can't stand you right now! I can't stand being in here!"

"Beth, where are you going? It's two degrees out."

"I need some air. I need to think."

"But it's almost midnight," Andrew said. Beth looked him in the eye.

"Then merry Christmas," she said.

And with that she was out the door and into the stormy Christmas Eve night.

Andrew went to the window and looked down just in time to see Beth turn up snow-covered 89th Street. He hurried to the door and put his overcoat back on.

There really was no choice. He had to go after her.

CHAPTER SEVEN

*A*s Beth stomped into the blustery Manhattan night, she felt the hot tears freeze on her cheeks. She had no idea where she was going; she just had to keep moving, as if distance would somehow ease the sharp pain of betrayal.

She arrived at the corner of 88th and Third and hesitated. Which way now? She hadn't a clue.

She had always loved a white Christmas, and here she was standing like a lonely snow angel with no particular place to be. The grand city seemed lovely and serene, but Beth felt no peace. Her heart was in shambles, her stomach tied up in knots. A wave of nausea washed over her, and a foreboding shudder rolled down her. She wanted to run from it—whatever *it* was—but knew there was no escape.

Then she heard a dog bark. An unusual sound in New York City. Why on earth would a dog be out on a night like this?

Then it hit her. She knew that bark.

"Lulu?"

Beth spotted Mrs. Applebee's furry little drifter standing in the middle of Third Avenue, a wary tail wagging in Beth's direction. The pup had found a friend amidst the storm.

"Hey, you crazy girl. What are you doing out here?" Beth cautiously stepped out into the street, careful not to spook the wayward doggy.

A block away, Andrew rounded the corner and stopped to get his bearings. He looked down, and there in the freshly fallen snow, he found his answer: Beth-sized footprints heading up the sidewalk.

He'd only tracked a few paces when he saw her, crouched in the middle of the deserted street, her back to him. He saw movement, a fluff of white fur, heard a yelp. It was that darn dog again.

"Beth?"

She didn't hear him. She was too far away. Then, in a terrifying instant, he caught a glimpse of a taxi flying down Third Avenue, high beams glaring. Surely she'd see it. She had to see it.

But she was still hunched over the dog, oblivious to the danger racing toward her. *"Beth!"*

The cab was closing fast, terribly fast. Beth stood up, cradling the dog in her arms. She turned toward the blinding lights at the moment the cabbie spotted her. He laid down hard on the horn, a wasted gesture that was too little, far too late. For a moment, Beth stood frozen in the headlights as over three thousand pounds of compact metal bore down on her.

Brakes screamed. Andrew screamed. The cab fishtailed wildly, then slammed into Beth at forty miles an hour.

In the moment before impact, Beth tossed the helpless dog

out of harm's way. Lulu hit the snowy pavement with a whimper and scampered safely away just as the front bumper of the taxi slammed into Beth, sending her flying backward down the street. The thud was sickening and horrific, and Andrew knew immediately his wife was hit dead-on.

"Beth!" Andrew ran to her, sobbing. "Beth . . . Beth!"

He turned her over, cradled her head on his lap, as the horror-stricken cabbie jumped out of his taxi and ran toward the huddled figures in the street. When the driver saw Beth's broken body, his knees buckled and he collapsed, his anguished face in his hands.

Half a dozen people emerged from the storm, drawn like snow zombies to the scene of the tragedy. "Somebody call an ambulance," Andrew shouted.

A middle-aged man quickly moved to stop oncoming traffic while a young woman dialed 911 on her cell.

Andrew took Beth's wrist, tried to feel for a pulse, but he was trembling so badly he couldn't hold her arm still. Her eyes were closed, her lips set in a soft half smile. Andrew pulled her into his arms and cried, "Please, God, no. Please don't take my wife."

CHAPTER EIGHT

*H*alf an hour later, Andrew sat on a cold leather couch in the waiting room of the hospital ER and watched a tiny artificial Christmas tree flicker. "I'll Be Home for Christmas" played low over the speakers. Beth's favorite Christmas song.

A pair of forbidding swinging doors separated the waiting room from the trauma center, where a medical team worked desperately to save his wife's life. Andrew stared at the doors, closed his eyes, and tried to pray. He remembered what his grandmother used to say: "Just pray to know that God is in control, and then let it go."

He tried hard to concentrate, but his thoughts swirled wildly and he couldn't focus.

Andrew remembered reading somewhere that if you visualized something hard enough, you could bring it into existence, make the thing you desired come true. He wasn't exactly what you'd call a spiritual man, but at this darkest of moments, Andrew Farmer was visualizing for all he was worth. He needed Beth to be okay. He needed his wife back.

"Mr. Farmer?" The ER doc stood over him, her wrinkled green scrubs spattered with blood. She appeared to be in her mid-forties, and her practiced poker face gave nothing away.

Andrew stood up. Maybe his visualization had worked. The news would be good. It had to be good.

"Mr. Farmer, I'm Dr. Atkinson. Can we speak privately, please?"

Andrew looked around at the waiting room. They were all alone. "This is private enough," he said.

The doctor nodded and peeled off her surgical gloves. "Mr. Farmer, I'm afraid the news isn't good. Your wife's injuries are just too severe. We did everything we could. I'm so sorry."

Andrew stared at her as if waiting for the punch line. He searched her face for a sign of something more, something hopeful. But the anguished look in the doctor's eyes told him all he needed to know.

There would be no Christmas miracle. Beth hadn't made it.

Andrew cautiously approached the gurney where Beth's frail body lay covered in a sheet. Her face was calm and serene and appeared strangely unmarked by the violent collision. He pulled up a chair, took her lifeless hand, and gave it a squeeze. Words of grief tumbled out in sobbing half syllables.

"I'm sorry, Beth. I'm so sorry. How could you die like this? Please, God, give me one more chance. Don't let her die thinking that I—"

Andrew stared at Beth's pale face. She was beautiful, even in death. A tear dripped from his chin onto her cheek. He gently wiped it off with his thumb. She was cold. So cold.

He wasn't sure how long he sat there, but at some point in the predawn hours of Christmas morning, a gentle hand on his shoulder told him it was time to go.

Despite a hospital security guard's offer to drive him home, Andrew opted to hoof the twelve blocks from the Lenox Hill Hospital to the apartment in Carnegie Hill. It was well after five in the morning when he staggered up to his street-side entry door. He fumbled in his pockets for the key, slipped it in the lock. But when he tried to turn it, just like he'd done a thousand and one times before, it wouldn't cooperate.

He pulled the key out, held it up in the security light for a closer look. There was the faded snatch of masking tape on it with Beth's handwriting: "Bldg. Key." He peered into the keyhole to see if maybe someone had broken something off in there. It seemed fine. He tried again. No go.

Andrew sagged in frustration. Of all times. He again checked the key to see if maybe it had been bent or damaged. It looked okay. He peered through the glass looking for any sign of life in the building stairwell. Not a soul in sight. He even checked the address on the door just in case, in his mental stupor, he'd stumbled up to the wrong building.

No, he was definitely in the right place.

Andrew stepped over to the buzzer panel and, in a fit of

frustration, started pushing apartment buttons one by one. Nobody picked up, even though he knew almost everybody in the building had to be home in bed.

"Perfect," he said. The worst night of his life had somehow found a way to get even worse.

Then, reflected in the glass door, an orange glow captured his attention. He turned and looked for the source. Across the street, a lighted window sign read "Locksmith."

Andrew stared at it for a moment. There was no locksmith across the street from his apartment. There had been a coffee shop there when they'd moved to the neighborhood, but it had closed, and there'd been a "For Lease" sign in the window ever since.

Was it possible a new business moved in without his even noticing? Besides, how could a locksmith afford a storefront in this neighborhood unless they sold fourteen-karat gold keys a dozen at a time? And beyond that, even if there were a locksmith shop across the street, why in heaven's name would they be open at 5:00 a.m. on Christmas morning?

Andrew looked up and down the empty street and shrugged. It wasn't like he had a plethora of options, after all.

"Hello?"

Andrew pushed open the squeaky-hinged door and stepped inside. It was a tiny mom-and-pop shop that looked like it'd been torn out of a page from 1965. *Shops like this don't exist anymore,* Andrew thought. *Particularly not in Manhattan.*

The darkened room was scattered with table vises, files, and sanders, an old weathered workbench. A vintage Christmas calendar with a rosy-cheeked Santa drinking a Coca-Cola was tacked to the wall.

"Hello?" Andrew said. "Anybody here?"

"Close the door!" a man's voice said. "I can't afford to heat all of Gotham."

Andrew pushed the door closed behind him and turned to see that the voice had emerged from a back room and was now watching him from behind the counter. The man was wearing work coveralls and had a file in his hand that moved back and forth in rhythm as he filed down a key. He was black, of average build, and stood about six feet tall. At first glance, Andrew thought he was a very young man, maybe in his twenties, but upon closer examination he reconsidered and put him somewhere in his late forties or early fifties. His eyes were clear and penetrating.

The man looked him over, as if browsing through Andrew's mind, searching for something. For a moment, Andrew knew a split second of intense self-awareness, as if he had glimpsed a vision of himself that was wholly separate from his mortal existence.

A shiver of fear shot through Andrew's veins, and he tried to turn and leave. But his legs wouldn't respond to his brain's command.

"So how can I help you?" the man said. "I'm very busy."

"I live in the apartment across the street," Andrew said. "I'm locked out."

The man glared at him. "So what do you need me for?"

Andrew glared back. "I need help."

The man nodded slowly as if Andrew had stumbled onto the answer of an obscure trivia question. "So you do."

"Well, can you help me or not?"

The locksmith nodded again. "I believe I can. That is, if you want my help."

"I'm here, aren't I?" Andrew said. "Now, if you could just follow me over to my apartment—"

"Sorry to hear about your wife," the locksmith said.

Andrew tensed. "How do you know about my wife?"

"Word spreads quickly. Lovely lady, Beth. Too bad you didn't appreciate her."

Andrew tried to quell the churning in his stomach. "Who are you?"

The man smiled. "Name's Lionel."

"That doesn't help me much," Andrew said.

"What were you thinking? Messin' around with that woman in Chicago?"

Andrew felt the blood rush to his face. "I wasn't messing around . . ." He took a step closer to the counter. "What do you want from me?"

"What do *you* want from *me*?" Lionel said.

"I told you. I want to get into my apartment!"

Lionel chuckled. "Not that. I'm talking about your prayer, Andrew. Remember?"

"What prayer?" Andrew said.

"Back at the hospital. You prayed for another chance with Beth. So here I am." Andrew stared at him. "What's the matter, Andrew? Don't you believe in prayer?"

"I . . . don't know what to believe," Andrew said.

"If you don't believe in your prayer, then why did you pray?"

"Who knows?" Andrew said. "Maybe because I'm all out of options."

Lionel chuckled. "You and almost everybody else. Most people turn to a higher power only as a last resort. Pity you have so little faith."

"You know what I think?" Andrew said. "I think you're crazy." He turned to leave, but Lionel's next words stopped him in his tracks.

"The night your mother died you couldn't sleep, so you climbed out of your bedroom window and sat on the roof. You stared up at the sky and said something. Do you remember what you said?"

Andrew knew exactly what he'd said. He had relived that moment thousands of times. But he wanted to hear the locksmith say it.

"God, if you're really up there . . . ," Lionel prodded.

". . . then show me a sign," Andrew said.

Lionel nodded. "At that moment you saw something in the sky. What was it, Andrew?"

"A shooting star," Andrew said. In his mind, he saw the star's spectacular death arc across the black sky.

"You had your sign," Lionel said, "but you were so full of pain and bitterness you refused to believe it."

"You aren't just a locksmith, are you?" Andrew said.

"Very perceptive." Lionel ran the rasp across the key again. "But in a way, that's exactly what I am. I'm offering you a key. I'm prepared to give you a chance to make things right."

"What do you mean?"

"A gift. A rare, once-in-a-lifetime opportunity."

"What gift?" Andrew said.

Lionel finished filing the key. "*You* get three days. *We* get Beth."

"I don't understand," Andrew said.

"Let me finish," Lionel said. "Then you'll be given the opportunity to either accept or reject the gift. If you reject it, then I go on my way, and this meeting never happened. You play golf, right?"

Andrew nodded.

"Then consider this a mulligan."

"A mulligan," Andrew said.

"A do-over. A chance to set things right. If you accept the gift, then when you wake up in the morning, it will again be Friday, December 22. You'll have the past three days to live all over again. Beth will be alive, with no memory of what happened. You can spend those three days any way you wish, but you have an assignment. You have to prove to Beth that you truly love her."

"And what happens Sunday night?" Andrew said.

"At 11:58 p.m. Christmas Eve, Beth must keep her date with that speeding taxi," Lionel said. "She will die all over again just like before. Same place, same time. I'm sorry, Andrew, but that is her fate."

Andrew jutted out his chin. "Well, what if I won't let that happen? What if I change the past?"

Lionel smiled as if he fully expected this response. "If you try to change Beth's destiny or interfere in any way, those days will be gone as if they never happened. If you want my advice, Andrew, take the offer. Give your wife a proper send-off. She deserves it.

Besides, do you know how many people would kill for a chance like this?"

Andrew stared at him, his thoughts twisting in all directions.

"So, do we have a deal?" Lionel said.

Andrew hesitated for a moment, then slowly nodded.

"Good," Lionel said. "Now go home. And try not to screw this up."

Andrew stared mutely at this strange figure of a man wearing coveralls. He had a million and one questions, but hadn't a clue where to begin.

Lionel winked at him. "Oh, right, one more thing." He tossed Andrew the key he'd been so meticulously filing. Andrew snatched it out of the air, studied it in the palm of his hand. It was a peculiar, ornate gold key that looked like it was made to open some pirate's treasure chest. He was quite sure it wouldn't fit his building door.

When he looked up, Andrew was no longer standing in the dingy locksmith shop. He was back outside his building, alone in the cold.

He took the oversized gold key and slipped it in the door lock, fully expecting that it wouldn't fit.

One click. It turned easily, and the door swung open.

Andrew looked over his shoulder at the shop across the street. The lights were off and the shades were drawn.

A "Closed" sign hung in the door.

CHAPTER NINE

*T*he traffic noise from the street below stirred Andrew from a restless sleep. He lay motionless for a few moments, listening. It was Christmas Day, a time when the traffic should be sparse, yet the city noises sounded as if it were any other workday. The sunlight seeping through the blinds told him that the storm had passed them by, making the weather folks wrong yet again.

Then the events of the previous night crashed full force into his mind. The accident. Beth's horrific death. His tearful good-bye at the hospital. The walk back. The strange locksmith with a most unusual proposition.

Three days.

He rushed to the window and cracked the blinds. No snow on the ground, not even a trace from the previous night's blizzard.

Andrew took a calming breath and looked back at the empty bed. Maybe everything that happened last night, from after he left the hospital to when he crawled into bed, was just an illusion, a hallucination. It was possible. Grief did strange things to people.

But what about the snowstorm? Surely he wasn't mistaken about that. Surely that was real.

The truth welled up and choked him. Beth was gone, and nothing in the world could bring her back. He sat on the edge of the bed and tried to breathe. He had to keep moving, had to find a way to go on.

And he had things to do. An obituary, a memorial service. He had to phone Beth's relatives in Florida. He desperately wanted to crawl back under the covers and hide from all of it.

But if the situation were reversed, Beth wouldn't be moping around, wallowing in self-pity. She'd have her cry, and then she'd pull herself together and give her late husband a send-off for the ages.

He smiled at the thought. If only the situation *could* be reversed, he'd jump at the chance.

Then, from somewhere in the apartment, he heard music. The stereo was playing Bing Crosby.

Happy holiday,
Happy holiday,
While the merry bells keep ringing
May your every wish come true.

Andrew stood up and slowly moved toward the sound. How could there be music? Beth must have set the alarm timer on the CD player.

As he stepped into the living room, he heard the pop and crackle of burning timber. There was a fire in the fireplace, a couple of extra logs in the firewood holder. Andrew thought for a moment, tried to retrace his steps from the night before. Could he have lit a fire and not remembered doing it? He knew he hadn't; he wouldn't have.

It made no sense. Maybe there were still embers from the previous evening—maybe they'd somehow reignited. If that was the case, why did the firewood look fresh? Nothing about the morning made sense. His heart quickened as he looked at the window. Something was missing.

The corner where Beth had set up that pitiful little Christmas tree—empty. No lights and bulbs, no popcorn strands or falling needles. No Charlie Brown tree.

But how could that be? He specifically remembered leaning down and unplugging the lights just before he'd staggered off to bed. The tree had been there. He had placed it there himself on Friday evening. Beth had stood in that corner and quietly decorated as he hurriedly packed for Chicago. She had been standing by its glowing branches in the window as he climbed into the cab.

But now it was gone. Maybe someone was playing a cruel trick on him. Or, even more disturbing, maybe his mind was slipping. Could this be some kind of post-traumatic stress brought on by Beth's death?

Andrew walked over to the CD player and switched it off as a familiar scent hit him. Perfume. *Beth's* perfume. Then he heard footfalls on the stairs, steps heading down the hall toward the apartment.

Someone is coming.

A moment later, the clatter of keys and the sound of one slipping into the lock. Andrew stared stupidly at the door as the bolt turned, the door pushed open, and Beth stepped through.

She was dressed in her woolen winter coat, ski hat, and gloves; her cheeks were kissed rosy by the cold. She looked wonderful. Andrew gaped at her as she removed the keys from the door, closed it behind her. In her arms she carried a brown bag from the bagel shop on the corner. Under her arm she gripped a copy of the *New York Times.* "Hey!" she said. "You're up."

She set the bag and newspaper on the kitchen counter, stepped over to him, and turned the backs of her cold hands against his cheeks. "Feel."

Andrew stared at her smiling face and struggled to get control of himself. He watched in silence as she peeled off her wrappings and hung them by the door.

"Where were you?"

"I went for bagels," Beth said. "It's so beautiful out. Not a cloud in the sky."

As Beth moved into the kitchen to start breakfast, Andrew went to the kitchen counter and unfolded the morning paper. *Friday, December 22.*

Andrew breathed a sigh of deep relief as the obvious truth sank in. It had been a dream. An incredibly vivid and realistic dream, but a dream nevertheless.

He smiled, tossed the paper back on the counter, and wrapped his arms around Beth from behind. "Good morning, beautiful."

Beth turned to him. "Whoa," she said. "Where did that come from?"

"I don't know." Andrew shrugged. "Can't a guy call his wife beautiful once in a while?"

Beth shot him a quizzical look. "Sure. Anytime."

"I had the funkiest dream last night," Andrew said. "Seemed so real."

Beth went back to her breakfast prep. "Speaking of funky, look what I found in the key tray this morning." She held up the ornate key that Lionel had given Andrew. "Is this yours?"

Andrew stared at the key in her hand, his momentary relief sucked right out of him. He finally managed a nod.

"Where did you get it?"

Andrew felt his stomach clench. "I, um, found it on the street."

"Well, it certainly is unusual," Beth said. She placed the key on the counter and turned back to breakfast.

Andrew swallowed hard, his guts churning. It wasn't a dream after all. And if it wasn't a dream, that meant the clock was ticking.

"Three days," he said.

CHAPTER TEN

We have to get our tree," Beth said. "I was thinking you could meet me after work today."

Andrew's body was sitting across from Beth at the breakfast table, but his mind was miles away, running on adrenaline. He simply couldn't focus. There was too much to process, too much to try to figure out.

He'd only managed one tiny bite of bagel, and Beth had been forced to intervene to stop him from pouring orange juice on his cereal. Food was the last thing on his mind at the moment, and getting a Christmas tree ranked only a half notch above.

"Earth to Andrew," Beth said.

Andrew looked at her as if suddenly realizing she was there. "Yeah, sure," he said.

Beth smiled. "What did I say?"

"We need to get a tree."

"So? Can you meet me after work?"

Andrew noticed a dabble of cream cheese on her upper lip and suddenly wanted to kiss it away. "No," he said.

Beth winced. He hadn't meant to bark it out like that. "I mean, I have a better idea. A *much* better idea."

"Oh?" Beth said. "This I have to hear."

Andrew took her hands. "How about if I don't go to work at all?"

"Who are you?" Beth said. "And what have you done with my real husband?"

"I'm serious," Andrew said. "I want this to be the greatest Christmas weekend of your life, the most amazing three days of our marriage."

Beth gave him a dubious look, and he pressed on. "Really, Beth. This weekend is all about *you*. Whatever you want, whatever you need, I will do everything in my power to provide it."

"You're kidding, right?"

"I mean it. I want you to think very, very hard. Where would you like to go this weekend? And think big. We can go anywhere in the world. Paris. Tahiti. Name it, and I'll book it."

"What about your work?"

"Forget about my work. I've got vacation days stacked up since 2010."

"There's a reason for that, honey," Beth said. "Work is the most important thing in the world to you."

"*You're* the most important thing in the world to me," Andrew said. "Maybe I haven't always acted that way, but I'm trying to change. Won't you help me?"

Andrew's iPhone vibrated on the table. Beth picked it up, saw who was calling.

"Your office," she said. "Knew this was too good to be true."

Andrew took the phone from her and switched it off. Beth

gave an exaggerated gasp. "Honey, did you hit your head or something? Or—I know—you were visited by the Ghost of Christmas Yet to Come!"

Andrew smiled. "Kind of. The point is, it's Christmas, and I'm spending the weekend with my wife. So, have you decided where you want to go?"

"Let me be sure I have this straight," Beth said. "You'll take me anywhere in the world I want to go? My choice?"

"Anywhere," Andrew said.

Penn Station was teeming with holiday travelers. Andrew and Beth worked their way through a bustling terminal decked out with a twenty-foot Christmas tree, poinsettias, and giant plastic candy canes.

Beth tugged Andrew over to the big black departure board near the top of the escalators. He watched his wife scan the dozens of destinations. She seemed positively giddy.

"I don't think we can get to Paris from here," Andrew said.

"Good," Beth said. "Because I don't want to go to Paris." She pointed up to the board. "There it is! My dream destination." Andrew followed her finger and spotted two familiar words.

"River Falls?" he said. "Seriously, Beth?"

Beth smiled at him and took his hand. "Seriously. You said *my choice*, and that's where I want to go."

Andrew smiled. "I said think big. A trip to the library's bigger than this."

"You made the rules, buddy."

"Yes, I did."

"Okay, then. Stop your grousing and let's go!" Andrew shook his head and stepped up to the ticket booth. "Two tickets to River Falls, please."

A light snow was falling on River Falls, Pennsylvania, when the three o'clock train from New York City pulled into the station. Beth was the first one on the platform when the doors opened, leaving Andrew to grab the luggage.

"Andrew, hurry!"

A moment later Andrew lumbered out, toting the bags. He watched as Beth performed a joyful pirouette on the snow-dusted platform, Alice arriving in Wonderland. "I can't believe we're here!" she said. "Home. The sweetest spot on earth!"

Andrew forced a smile. River Falls was not such a sweet spot for him. When they moved to Manhattan, he shook the dust of this one-horse town off his feet and never looked back.

But Beth, who had never gotten over her homesickness, jumped at the chance to come home for Christmas. Suddenly Andrew felt guilty for not bringing her back before now.

Beth threw her arms around him. "Thank you for this!"

"You're welcome," Andrew said.

Lionel had told him that he couldn't change his wife's fate. But what if *she* could change it? What if Beth refused to go back to New York? What if she was nowhere near that street at 11:58 on Christmas Eve?

An ember of hope flickered into flame. Maybe there was a chance.

Beth let go of him and danced away. "C'mon, let's get checked in so we can go exploring!"

Ten minutes later the only taxi in town rolled up outside the River Falls Inn, a charming old three-story house that was converted to a bed-and-breakfast some fifty years back. The lethargic cab-driver hoisted his bulky frame out of the driver's seat with such effort it seemed as if he hadn't stood up in weeks. He shuffled slowly back to the trunk, being overly cautious of the ice patches. He groaned as he lifted out the luggage. Beth snatched the fare from Andrew and slipped it into the driver's hand, tacking on a ten spot for good measure.

"Here you go," she said. "Keep the change." The driver stared at the extra cash and then turned to stare at her.

"I know you," he said. "You're Beth McCarthy."

Beth beamed. "I am," she said. "What's your name?"

"Larry. Larry Miller."

"Larry! Of course! I didn't recognize you!" She gave him a hug. "Andrew, remember Larry? He was a freshman when we were seniors."

The truth was, Andrew didn't even come close to remembering him. But he stuck out his hand. "Hey there, Larry."

Larry nodded to Andrew and shook his hand, but his eyes stayed focused on Beth. "Beth, do you remember my fifteenth birthday?" the cabbie said. His eyes lit up, and a boyish grin spread across his homely face.

Beth thought for a moment. "Yes, I do. It was at your house. Your mom made spaghetti."

Larry's grin widened. "I invited pretty much everybody at school. You were the only one to show up."

"Really, Larry?" Beth said. "I don't remember that."

"It's true," the cabbie said. "My mother talked about you until the day she died. She said you were the kind of girl any guy would be lucky to marry. She said you had *class*."

Larry turned his gaze on Andrew. "I wasn't exactly Mr. Popularity in high school," he said. "But your wife here didn't care. She treated me like I was somebody." Larry handed the fare and tip back to Andrew. "This one's on me. You folks enjoy your stay, now. And if you need any more rides, you just call ole Larry."

"Thanks," Andrew said. He grabbed the bags as Larry tipped his hat to Beth.

"Good to see you again."

Beth smiled. "You too, Larry." Then Larry climbed back in his taxi and drove back toward the train station.

"That was sweet," Beth said.

"Yeah," Andrew said.

Beth snatched her suitcase from him. "Well, come on! Time's a wastin'."

Andrew forced a smile. "That it is," he said. "That it is."

CHAPTER ELEVEN

*B*eth McCarthy! The girl with the million-dollar smile." The inn's owner, Mr. Gibbons, beamed at Beth from behind the check-in counter.

"You're so sweet, Mr. Gibbons," Beth said. She nodded toward Andrew. "And it's Beth *Farmer* now."

"Oh, that's right," Gibbons said. "You married Emma and Henry Farmer's boy. You kids were two peas in a pod, if I remember."

Andrew glanced at his Rolex. "Yep," he said. "So, any vacancies?"

"Well, let's see . . ." The old innkeeper glanced back at the key rack on the wall. No plastic card keys for the River Falls Inn; it was strictly old-school brass dangling from the hooks. And there were plenty of them. Not exactly a holiday rush on rooms. "Appears to be wide open. What are you looking for?"

"The best room you have," Andrew said. "Preferably a suite. Presidential, if you have one. If not, anything with a sitting room. And we'd like the top floor."

Beth shot Andrew a look as Mr. Gibbons mulled it over. "Hmm, let's see . . ." The old man's face lit up. "How about room number three? The De Niro Suite."

"Robert De Niro stayed here?" Beth said.

Mr. Gibbons chuckled as if she'd just gotten off a good one. "Oh no. But a man who looked a good deal like him did once. All the ladies in town thought it really was De Niro and camped out on the front lawn. It was quite the to-do. The poor fella had to come out and show his driver's license to convince them otherwise."

Beth smiled and glanced at Andrew. "That's a great story."

Andrew didn't think so. He nervously tapped the counter. "We'll take it."

"Wow, great room!" Andrew said as he lugged the suitcases through the door of room number three. In reality, the room was no great shakes. Certainly no suite. He did a quick butt bounce off the bed. "Springy mattress. Just the way you like it."

"What is with you?" Beth said. "You're acting very strange."

"Strange?" Andrew said. "I'm not acting anything."

"Uh, yes, you are. 'Give us your best room. Top floor. Do you have a presidential suite?'"

"Beth, I just want you to be happy."

"Oh? Or is it more about Andrew Farmer the conquering hero returns home?"

"Beth, I don't know what—"

"Andrew, you left town, you've done well. Everybody knows it. You don't have to show off."

"I'm not showing off. I just want this to be the perfect weekend. That's all."

Beth gave him a dubious look. Andrew knew it was best to shift topics as quickly as possible. "Okay," he said. "What do you want to do? On the ride in I noticed they were setting up for some shindig in Town Square. You love that stuff."

"Andrew, it's not 'some shindig.' It's Candlelight Christmas. Don't you remember? We used to go together every year."

"Yeah, of course I remember," he said. "Didn't we have our first kiss there?"

Beth smiled and shook her head. "You really are a guy, aren't you? Our first kiss was at Susie Thompson's sweet sixteenth."

"Right. Now I remember. We were playing some game."

Beth started to unpack. "Truth or Dare," she said. "Bobby Mulligan dared you to kiss me."

Andrew began unloading his own bag. "I have a confession to make," he said. "I paid Mully off." Beth gave him a look, then grinned. It seemed Andrew had finally said the right thing. She went over and gave him a peck on the cheek.

"That one's for free."

Andrew rubbed his hands together. "So, what do you say we get out of here? Stretch our legs."

"Okay. Just give me a second to freshen up."

The moment Beth stepped into the bathroom and closed the door, Andrew collapsed onto the edge of the bed. He felt as if he'd just run a marathon. His heart was racing; he was sweating. The pretending-everything's-normal game was exhausting.

"Having fun yet?"

Andrew sprang up and whipped around to discover Lionel lounging on the bed, feet up, arms behind his head, a relaxed smile on his face. "You! You scared the—! What are you doing here?" Andrew said.

Lionel yawned. "Just checking in on you. You really need to chill out, my friend. All this stress is going to give you an ulcer."

"Stress? Stress? Yeah, I've got some stress. Who wouldn't, under these circumstances?"

Lionel chuckled. "I suppose you're right. So, have you figured out what to give her yet?"

"Give her? What are you talking about?"

"Beth's last Christmas present."

Andrew's agitation ramped up another notch. "Christmas present? How am I supposed to think about a Christmas present, knowing what I know? Knowing what's going to happen Sunday night at 11:58? Sorry if I don't have time to focus on shopping!"

"Well, I'd think—knowing what you know—you'd want to get her something nice, something special. Unlike the apron you got her last year. After all, it's your last shot."

Andrew pointed an angry finger at Lionel and whispered, "What? What is it I'm supposed to get her? Enough with the riddles. Just tell me!"

"Can't do that," Lionel said.

"Why not?"

"It's not for me to say."

Andrew started pacing the room. "Oh, right. Of course not! What is your function, anyway? Just for the record. I thought you angel-types were supposed to help us mere mortals. Isn't that your job?"

Lionel chuckled. "Never said I was an angel."

"Well, whatever you are. A spirit. A messenger. A goblin."

"Put some thought into the gift, Andrew. I'm sure it'll come to you."

"Oh, and by the way," Andrew said. "For your information, the apron said 'The Boss' on it. It was supposed to be a joke."

"Beth didn't think it was funny."

"And how do you know that?" Andrew said. "Oh, right. You're an—"

"Andrew, who are you talking to out there?"

Andrew whipped around toward the bathroom door just as Beth emerged.

"Nobody! Just me!"

Beth gave him a curious look. Andrew glanced back at the bed. Lionel was gone. "I was just . . . talking to . . . myself," he said. "About . . . how much fun we're going to have."

Beth shook her head. "Somebody needs some fresh air. *Vamos.*" She grabbed her coat and scarf and headed out the door.

Andrew stared at the empty bed. The spot where Lionel had just been lounging was completely wrinkle-free.

"C'mon, slowpoke," Beth called back through the open door. "While we're still young."

Downtown River Falls looked like an old-fashioned Currier and Ives Christmas card. The shop windows were spruced up with fake frost, twinkling lights, and various North Pole—themed displays. Andrew and Beth strolled hand in hand along a sidewalk bustling with last-minute shoppers. Beth had a skip in her step, calling out, "Merry Christmas," or "Happy Holidays," to everyone she passed.

"It's still here!" Beth said. She stopped suddenly and gestured to a tiny shop across the square. "I can't believe it's still here!" She took Andrew by the arm and tugged him across the street and through the jingling door of a quaint little shop called Forever Christmas.

The inside of the store smelled of hot apple cider and gingerbread. Bing Crosby's "White Christmas" crooned over the speakers. Beth's face glowed as she perused shelves and nooks and crannies filled with holiday-themed antiques and knick-knacks. "When I was little, this was my favorite place in the world," she said. "Whenever Mom brought me into town on errands, I'd slip away from her and come here. She always knew where to find me."

Andrew lifted an old hardback book from a shelf, read the cover. "*The Lost Christmas* by Alistair Whitman. Set right here in River Falls."

Beth took the book from him, opened to the copyright page. "Andrew. It's a first edition! Who would have guessed that one day you'd grow up to be his agent?"

"Yeah," Andrew said. "And now he's writing a sequel. *The Lost Christmas Revisited*. Title needs work, I know."

"No kidding." Beth laughed, and then her gaze lit on something perched on a table a few feet away. It was an old music box, a finely crafted antique made of rosewood and polished to a high shine. It depicted a winter scene with miniature skaters on a frozen country pond.

She hovered over the music box for a moment, gave the winding key a turn, and the box began to plunk out a leisurely version of "The Nutcracker Suite" by Tchaikovsky. The little wintry-clad figurines skated across a tiny pond.

Beth watched the miniature scene beneath the glass, then whispered a single syllable: "Wow."

"Home, sweet home," Beth said. After half an hour of browsing in Forever Christmas, Andrew and Beth strolled the four blocks to the old Farmer family home tucked away on a quiet tree-lined street called Dogwood Lane. The house was a majestic Victorian built near the end of the nineteenth century and restored at least a half dozen times since. As Andrew stood on the sidewalk by the front gate, the memories came flooding back.

"A real blast from the past, huh?" Beth said.

"Yeah." Andrew tugged on her hand. "Why don't we leave it there?"

"Oh, come on," Beth said. She looped her arm through his. "There were good times here too. I remember those long talks with your mom after my mom died. She was so kind to me, took me in like I was her own daughter. And those gin rummy games with your dad on the front porch. He always let me win."

"Good ole Dad," Andrew said.

"Remember the time he surprised you with a train set for

Christmas? You two stayed up for hours on Christmas Eve playing with it."

"Right," Andrew said. "And then the next morning when I went to wake him up to play some more, he was gone. Didn't see him for a month after that."

Beth gave him a playful pout. "You know, you're a real 'glass half empty' guy, Andrew Farmer."

"So I've heard."

Beth pulled Andrew down to the sidewalk with her. "Look!" There, in a concrete square reminiscent of Grauman's Chinese Theatre, were two small handprints in the cement, and above them, the inscription *Beth Loves Andy*.

Beth smiled. "I remember when we did this." She took Andrew's hand, placed it over his old print, and put her hand over hers.

Andrew jerked his hand away. "They don't fit anymore," he said.

All the joy drained from Beth's face. She stood up; the magic of the moment vanished.

A man in a wool hat and plaid shirt came around from the back of the house. "Can I help ya?"

"We were just taking a stroll down memory lane," Beth said. "My husband grew up in this house."

A wave of recognition swept over the homeowner's face. He took a step forward to get a better look at his visitors.

"Andrew Farmer? And . . . Beth McCarthy?" Andrew and Beth nodded in unison.

"Well, hello!" the homeowner said. "It's so good to see you!" He stepped up to them and thrust out his hand.

"It's me. Mitch Foster! Remember? Got a real bad case of poison ivy on our senior class trip."

"Itchin' Mitchin'?" Andrew and Beth said in unison.

Mitch laughed. "Yep, that's me."

"Wow," Beth said. "How are you?"

"Just fine and dandy, thank you very much. Haven't had poison ivy since."

"That's good," Andrew said. He hoped this little reunion would be short-lived.

"Hey, why don't you two come inside?" Mitch said. "Megan would love to see you!"

"Megan?" Beth said. "Not Megan Ward?"

"One and the same," Mitch said.

"I didn't know you two married," Beth said.

"Yep. Together forever. Just like you two."

Andrew made an all-too-obvious glance at his watch. "We'd like to, Mitch, but we're really short on—"

Beth put a hand on Andrew's arm. "We've got plenty of time. Thanks, Mitch. We'd love to come in for a visit."

"I just love what you've done with the place," Beth said. Mitch and his pretty auburn-haired wife, Megan, beamed with pride. They'd obviously put a good deal of time and effort into the renovation. "I especially love the wood floors."

Beth glanced over at Andrew. He was doing his best to look interested, but he wasn't much of an actor.

Megan smiled at Andrew. "Who knew all this wood was hiding beneath that green shag carpet?"

Andrew shrugged. "Who knew?"

Beth moved to the Foster family photos lining the fireplace mantel. "And these are your children? They're beautiful."

"Katie's eleven and Tyler's eight," Mitch said. "They're going to be so excited when they find out you were here."

"Oh yes," Megan said. "You two are neighborhood legends. I mean, your names are everywhere. The trees, the fence, the cement—"

"So, what about you guys?" Mitch said. "Do you have children?"

Beth and Andrew exchanged an awkward look. Tricky territory. Beth managed a smile. "No," she said. "Not yet."

"You have to stay for dinner," Megan said. "So the kids can meet you."

"I'd love to!" Beth said.

She looked at her husband and knew she'd spoken too soon. For Andrew, the memories of his childhood home were anything but warm and fuzzy. She felt a wave of sympathy for him.

"You know," Beth said, "on second thought—"

Andrew cut her off. "Sounds great. Nothing like a home-cooked meal."

"Great!" Mitch said. As Megan and Mitch headed back to the kitchen, Beth sidled over to Andrew.

"You sure?"

"Yeah," he said. "This is your weekend. Your wish is my command."

Beth gave him a kiss on the cheek. "If you decide it's too much for you, just let me know and we'll go."

"Don't worry," Andrew said. "I'll be fine."

Dinner was in the same dining room where Andrew ate many a childhood meal with his mother. As he sat around the long, cherry dining room table with Beth and the Foster family, he could almost imagine his mother sitting in the same spot where Mitch was now. He remembered how she worked so hard to be cheerful even when her world was falling apart, even when she felt utterly hopeless.

He closed his eyes for a beat and could almost hear her voice asking him about his day, peppering him with questions about his mundane schoolboy life, discussing any and every subject under the sun, anything to avoid the elephant that wasn't sitting in the room. *Where's Dad? Why is he gone again? Who's he with? When will he be home?*

"You guys still skate out on Waller's Pond?" Andrew broke out of his momentary trance. Beth was talking to Mitch and Megan's kids. He noticed Tyler struggling to sit still under his mother's watchful gaze. His older sister, Katie, seemed to be thoroughly enchanted by Beth.

"All the time," Katie said.

"So did we," Beth said. "Some of the best memories of my childhood. Right, Andrew?"

Andrew looked at her as if to be sure she was speaking to him. "Uh, yes. Great memories."

"It's fun," Katie said. "Tyler's a little scared, though."

"I am not!" Tyler said. He gave his sister a kick under the table, and she retaliated.

"I don't get to skate so much anymore," Beth said. "I miss it. You know what I wish? Been sort of a dream of mine for a long time."

"What?" Katie and Tyler said in unison.

"I'd like to skate at Rockefeller Center someday. Just me, all alone on the ice beneath that big Christmas tree."

Andrew looked at Beth. She'd never mentioned this dream before.

"So, Andrew," Megan said. "Sounds like you've been really successful. I can't imagine what it's like being a big-time literary agent. Lots of wheeling and dealing, I'll bet."

Andrew dabbed his chin with his napkin. The last thing he wanted to do was talk about work. "It has its moments," he said.

"I'm just amazed we're here at all," Beth said. "Andrew's usually much too busy for spontaneous holiday trips. I'm beginning to think it was divine intervention."

Andrew did a spit-take and nearly knocked over his water glass. "Whoa. Sorry."

"You all right, Andrew?" Mitch said.

"Yeah, sorry. Guess I'm all thumbs this evening."

After dinner, Andrew retreated to the den with Mitch while Beth and Megan double-teamed the dishes in the kitchen.

Kicking back in his favorite recliner, Mitch looked over at Andrew on the couch and smiled. "Andy Farmer. Can't believe you're my guest in your old living room."

Andrew glanced at the clock on the fireplace mantel. Time was his enemy, and with each minute spent listening to Mitch wax nostalgic, he was inching ever closer to 11:58 p.m. Christmas Eve. It wasn't that Mitch was bad company, it was just Andrew found it nearly impossible to concentrate on anything his old schoolmate was saying. What he really wanted to do was run into the kitchen, grab his wife, and pull her out the door. But instead he said, "Yep, Mitch, hard to believe."

Tyler shouted from upstairs, "Dad! There's no toilet paper!"

"Cavalry's coming, sport!" Mitch called back. Mitch rose out of his chair. "Duty calls." Andrew waited until Mitch had gone upstairs and then let out a long breath. His stomach was tied in knots, his heart pounding. He headed for the kitchen to check on Beth.

As he drew near the kitchen's swinging door, he stopped. He could clearly hear the conversation going on as Beth and Megan washed dishes. He peered through the crack in the door and could see them at the sink.

"I didn't even like Mitch in high school," Megan said. "I thought he was a nerd." She rinsed a plate, handed it to Beth to dry. "Then I came home from college one Christmas and ran into him at a party. He seemed different. He made me laugh, and before I knew it, I was in love." Megan chuckled at the memory. "But who am I to tell you about love? You married your childhood sweetheart."

Andrew noticed Beth had stopped drying the dishes. She just stood there staring straight ahead. "Beth?" Megan said. A tear rolled down Beth's cheek. "Honey? What's wrong?"

"I'm sorry," Beth said. "It's just that . . . well, Andrew and I have been having problems for a long time. We don't really talk about them."

"What problems? I mean, if you don't mind me asking."

Beth's eyes filled with tears. "Things used to be so good between us, so easy and natural. But in the last few years, we've been slowly drifting apart, and lately it seems to have gotten worse. Andrew's hardly ever home, and when he is, we never talk. He never even looks at me anymore. Not like he used to. You know what I mean?"

Megan nodded. "Beth, all marriages go through rough patches."

"It's not that, Megan. It's something more. Something deeper. And then this morning, out of the blue, he's suddenly paying attention to me, treating me like he used to, like I'm special to him again." Beth looked into Megan's eyes. "Like he cares."

"Well, that's great!" Megan said. "Maybe he's coming around."

"It just doesn't seem . . . real," Beth said. "It seems forced. I don't know, Megan. I used to believe in true love and forever and all that stuff, but now I'm not so sure. To be honest, I really don't think Andrew loves me anymore." Beth started to softly sob. Megan took her in her arms, comforting her.

"It's okay, Beth. It'll all work out."

The eavesdropping Andrew stood dumbstruck on the other side of the kitchen door. He was in trouble. Big trouble. The love of his life no longer trusted him, no longer believed in him.

Then it struck him with a sudden painful conviction: Beth had died thinking that he'd betrayed her, that he no longer loved her.

He was failing at his one chance to make things right.

And in the background, the grandfather clock chimed eight thirty.

CHAPTER TWELVE

As the church bell tolled nine, a light snow fell on the packed River Falls Town Square. The whole town had come out for an age-old local tradition. Every December 22, for the past seventy years, local citizens had gathered for a candlelight ceremony.

At nine o'clock, as the church bell rang, River Falls residents would leave their homes and make their way to the town center, each carrying a lighted candle. The effect of hundreds of townsfolk walking quietly through the streets with their candles was surreally beautiful and deeply moving. The holiday custom began during the early dark days of World War II as a way to honor and remember those local soldiers fighting in far-off lands.

As Beth, Andrew, and the Foster family carried their candles from the house on Dogwood Lane to Town Square for the candlelight ceremony, Andrew stole a look at his wife. He couldn't seem to get her kitchen confession out of his mind. Did she really believe he no longer loved her? And if she did believe that, how could he possibly convince her otherwise before she met her fate on Sunday night? *You're supposed to be this hotshot agent,* he thought, *and you can't even sell your wife on the fact that you truly love her.*

He was tempted to pull Beth aside and confess everything. But what good would that do? She'd think he'd lost his mind. She'd probably call the men in the white coats to come get him.

And what if she did believe him? What then? Would *he* want to know if he were about to die? It was certain to put a damper on their final days together.

No, it was better she didn't know.

The short stroll to town seemed like forever as the swirl of anxious thoughts whipped around in Andrew's head. Finally, they rounded a corner, and there was the square lit up by the glow of several hundred candles.

"Wow," Beth said. "Breathtaking."

The Victorian bandstand was decked out with red bows, poinsettias, and green garlands. A majestic twenty-foot Fraser fir towered over the crowd. The tree was thick with handmade ornaments, strands of popcorn, and tinsel, but the lights had not been lit. Beth looped her arm through Andrew's. "Andrew, look! Isn't it beautiful?"

"We started a tradition a few years back," Mitch said. "Everyone in town hangs an ornament on the tree with their name on it. Helps us feel like one big family."

"That's lovely," Beth said.

Andrew nodded toward the big tree. "Guess somebody forgot to pay the electric bill."

Beth pulled him aside. "All this Christmas spirit too much for you?" she said.

"Are you kidding?" Andrew said. "I love this stuff."

Beth gave Andrew her "yeah, right" look just as Katie pulled her away.

"Beth, come with me!"

Andrew hung back, watched Beth and the others merge into the crowd near the bandstand. He heaved a frustrated sigh. The last thing he wanted to do was share Beth with a few hundred strangers.

"Isn't this wonderful!" Andrew turned to the sound of a woman's voice. She was standing so close to him she was practically rubbing up against him. Andrew gave her a look in hopes she'd get the hint and respect his personal space, but she didn't budge. He stepped away from her. She was short, less than five feet tall, and was bundled up snugly in coat, gloves, and a woolen hat pulled down over her ears.

"Yes," Andrew said. He didn't want to encourage her.

"I just love Christmas," she said. "Don't you, young man?"

"Sure," Andrew said. He looked around to see if she was with anyone, but she appeared to be alone.

"So how's it going?" the woman said.

"Fine," Andrew said.

"Is it?" she said. "Is it fine, Andrew? Because it doesn't appear to be going so well to me."

Andrew stared at her. She gave him a coy little smile and then pointed to a gold decorative pin stuck to her hat. It was in the shape of a key, the same key that Lionel had given him the night Beth died.

Andrew looked around. "Who are you?"

The old lady smiled. "I think you know the answer to that question. Perhaps, since things aren't going so well with Beth, I ought to remind you that you only have a little more than two days left to set things right. Doesn't time fly when you're having fun?"

"Fun?" Andrew said. "You think this is fun?" He leaned in close. "I need an extension."

The little lady cackled. "An extension? How precious you are! Now, I think you know that's not going to happen."

"If you're an angel, then you should be able to shake your magic wand or sprinkle your mystical powder—or whatever it is you do—and make it happen. Because I need more time."

"Oh, my dear. We don't carry wands or magic powder. We are bound by the rules of the universe, just like everybody else. Three days is all you've been granted. And it seems you've already wasted one of them."

Andrew put a hand on her arm. "Please," he said. "I need more time."

The woman patted his cheek affectionately. "You dear, dear boy. Christmas Eve, 11:58. Time will expire. It is your wife's destiny. Fate is fate. It cannot be trifled with."

Andrew looked away, spotted Beth in the crowd near the bandstand.

"Yeah, well, fate's not fair," he said.

"Have you given any thought to that gift?" the woman said.

Andrew brightened a little. "I've got something in mind. I'm going to surprise her."

The lady clapped her gloved hands. "Well, that's good news.

Beth likes surprises." She winked at him. "Well, surprises not named Kimberly, anyway."

Andrew glared at her. "Don't push your luck."

Just then Mayor Ed Drummond stepped up onto the bandstand and took the microphone. Behind him, the drummer in a five-piece band beat out a roll. The crowd applauded and cheered as the mayor held up his hand, gave them a big toothy politician's grin.

"Thank you, friends, and merry Christmas!" The crowd called back in kind. The mayor looked up at the towering tree, sitting there dark. "I'm sure you're all wondering why our tree isn't lit," he said.

A man called out from the crowd, "Hey, Mayor! You forget to pay the electric bill?" Laughter rolled through the crowd, and the mayor joined in.

"That guy stole my line," Andrew said. He turned to the old lady, but she was no longer beside him. She seemed to have vanished into thin air.

"Not quite, Harley," Mayor Drummond said. "Seems we have some kind of defect in the wiring. So far, nobody's been able to figure it out. But, lights or no lights, our band is cooking tonight, and they're taking requests!"

"'I'll Be Home for Christmas!'" Beth called out. Andrew smiled. He knew how much Beth loved that song.

The mayor searched for the voice, and he smiled as he recognized Beth. "Well, if it isn't the founder of my favorite charity, Best Buddies. Let's give Beth McCarthy a big welcome home!"

The crowd cheered. Mayor Drummond scanned the crowd. "Did Andy come with you?" Andrew weakly threw up a hand, but no one seemed to notice. He saw Beth look around to see if she could spot him, but their eyes never met.

"He's around here somewhere, Mr. Mayor!" she said. Andrew watched her whisper something to Megan, then saw Megan give her a sympathetic pat on the back.

He wondered what Beth had said.

Beth leaned against a tree and listened as the band kicked into a slow, sleepy version of "I'll Be Home for Christmas." The crowd joined in, swaying with their candles. Megan leaned into Beth. "I could go for some hot chocolate. Want some?"

"Sure," Beth said.

"Back in a jiffy," Megan said. Beth watched her friend head off through the crowd, then did another quick scan for Andrew. He seemed to have vanished into the night. Probably checking his e-mail or returning a call.

And then, out of the blue, an off-key voice blared from the big speakers. Andrew Farmer was singing a solo:

> *Christmas Eve will find me*
> *Where the love light gleams;*
> *I'll be home for Christmas,*
> *If only in my dreams . . .*

Beth put her hand to her mouth. She could scarcely believe what she was seeing. There was her husband onstage singing into the microphone, belting out a song, looking right at her, preening and gesturing like some cheesy lounge singer. Andrew really leaned into it, put it all on the line like King Karaoke.

What in the world? She had never known Andrew Farmer to do something so silly, so romantic.

The crowd joined in to help him out on the final line: *"If only in my dreams."*

As the song finished, Andrew stepped down from the stage, moved through the crowd to Beth, and took her in his arms. A movie moment. They kissed as the crowd repeated the last line and then broke into enthusiastic applause.

From the other side of the bandstand, an old woman watched the sweet scene and smiled. She casually flicked an index finger, as if flipping some invisible switch. The towering Christmas tree flickered to light. The crowd gasped and cheered.

Beth and Andrew didn't even notice. They were lost in each other's eyes and oblivious to everything else on earth. The old woman smiled and spoke to the sparkling, clear night sky.

"I love my job."

CHAPTER THIRTEEN

he old tower bell in the First Christian Church tolled ten as Andrew and Beth made their way back to the River Falls Inn. Beth looped her arm through his, rested her head on his shoulder. They had shared a connection back in the square, the first real connection in a long time. Was it possible that the Andrew Farmer she fell in love with so long ago had come back to her?

"Tonight is a moment for the ages," Beth said. "Andrew Farmer sings."

"Maybe I should audition for *American Idol*," Andrew said.

"Let's not push it." Beth squeezed his arm. "I can't believe you did that for me."

Andrew stopped, turned her to him, and looked deeply into her eyes. "Beth, I would do anything for you."

She reached up and caressed his face. There were so many things she wanted to say to him, but at that moment, what she really wanted was just to look at him, to enjoy the closeness that had for so long eluded them.

Mitch and Megan caught up to them. "Encore!" Mitch said.

"Sorry," Andrew said. "My singing career begins and ends tonight."

"Then it's a shame your father wasn't there to see it," Mitch said.

Beth cringed inwardly as she watched Andrew's face change. He tensed up, let go of her arm. She shot a warning look at Mitch, but he was oblivious and, besides, it was too late now.

"You know, I'm really tired," Beth said. "We'd better get going." She tugged on Andrew's arm to pull him away, but he held his ground.

"My father?" Andrew said.

Clueless, Mitch plunged ahead. "Well, I mean, it must be tough for him to get out these days."

Beth watched Andrew stiffen. "I wouldn't know."

Beth looked again for an exit. "Well, I guess we'll see you guys tomorrow," she said. She tried again to pull Andrew's hand, but he wasn't budging.

"Mitch, let's go," Megan said. She had obviously picked up on the awkward vibe, had seen Beth's face and knew Mitch had ventured into dangerous territory. She was doing her best to move her own husband in the opposite direction.

Mitch remained oblivious. "Have you dropped in to see him yet?"

"Mitch, he's in Arizona," Andrew said. "Or maybe Florida, last I heard."

Mitch gave Beth a puzzled look.

"Mitch, we really need to go," Megan said. She dug her fingernails into his arm.

"What's going on here?" Andrew said. Beth looked away. She didn't want to do this, at least not in the middle of the street. "Beth?"

Megan grabbed her husband's arm, dragged him away. "We're off to find the kids," she said. "See you guys later."

"Bye," Beth said. She could hear Megan giving Mitch a tongue lashing as they moved off. Beth looked at Andrew. His face was cold and distant again. The magical moment had turned on a dime.

"Beth?"

She looked him in the eye, drew a deep breath. "Andrew, your dad moved back to River Falls not long ago. He lives at the nursing home."

"How long?"

"Several months. Six maybe," Beth said.

"My father's been in River Falls for six months, and you . . . and nobody told me? What happened to his . . . to Connie or Callie or whatever her name is?"

"Carrie. She left him almost three years ago."

Andrew set his jaw. "Of course she did. It's called poetic justice."

"Andrew—"

"And how did you know he was here? Who told you?"

Beth took a beat. She really didn't want to tell him.

"Beth?"

"We've kept in touch."

"You've kept in touch? What, are you Facebook friends?"

"No, Andrew. More like pen pals. I've been writing your dad for years. He likes to know how you're doing. He likes to feel that he's still part of the family."

Andrew took a step back from her. "Part of the family? Oh, so *now* he wants to be part of the family? Well, that's just rich."

Beth could tell he wanted to walk away from her, but something kept him there. He took a few deep breaths. "Does he know we're here?"

Beth shook her head.

"Good. Let's keep it that way." With that, Andrew turned and walked up the street. Beth hesitated for a moment, then hurried to catch up to him.

"Andrew, he's sick. He has emphysema. He's really struggling."

"Two cartons a week. What do you expect?"

"Andrew, don't be that way. He's still your father."

"Beth, you know my history with that man. Where was he when Mom was dying? Huh? Where was he when she was calling his name, begging me to find him? Where was he at her funeral? He left us behind without so much as a glance in the rearview mirror, and I'm just supposed to act like it never happened?"

"I'm not asking you to forget, Andrew. But if you don't at least try and find a way to forgive him, your resentment will consume you. It will destroy you—destroy us."

Beth watched as Andrew tried to get a handle on his emotions.

Finally he spoke. "Beth, I'm sorry. It's just . . . well, the timing couldn't be worse."

"What do you mean?"

"I mean . . . we're here having our time together. *Our* time. The last thing we need is to have to deal with . . . this stuff."

"But, Andrew, he's your father."

"No, he's not. He's nothing to me. I'm sorry, Beth, but I hate that man. I don't ever want to see him again. Not ever."

Beth could see the deep pain in his eyes and decided it was

best not to press the issue. "Come on, then," she said. "Let's call it a night."

In the predawn hours of the next morning, Andrew sat in a chair and stared out the frosted window. A few feet away, Beth slept, her face peaceful and serene.

Andrew watched her, tried to imagine life without her. How long would it take until he was able to look at her picture again, read one of her old letters, glance through one of her countless scrapbooks? How long would it be until he stopped being choked with guilt? How long until he could move on?

His mind danced through his past, murky memories of his absent father mixed with happy glimpses of Beth. She'd always been there for him, and Lord knows he'd taken her for granted. He could almost hear Joni Mitchell singing "Big Yellow Taxi" in his head:

> *Don't it always seem to go*
> *That you don't know what you've got till it's gone . . .*

How could he have come to this point? And why had Fate chosen him for this cruel little experiment? Had others been given similar do-overs? If so, why hadn't he read about it in *Reader's Digest*?

He thought back to that moment in the Chicago hotel room with Kimberly. Did that really happen? Was the entire trip just an illusion? Or was *this* the illusion?

Beth stirred in bed, saw him sitting there, watching her. She spoke in a sleepy voice. "Please don't be mad at me."

"I could never be mad at you."

"In that case . . . want to hike out to Waller's Pond in the morning?"

Andrew smiled. He loved the way she slurred her words when she was really tired. "Sure," he said.

Beth patted the mattress. "Come to bed."

"I will soon," Andrew said. "I promise."

Beth rolled back over, fluffed the pillow, and drifted back to sleep. Andrew watched her for a moment and then withdrew into his tormented thoughts.

A little more than a mile from Town Square, Waller's Pond sat at the edge of an idyllic woodsy park that was a year-round favorite with picnickers, ice skaters, hikers, joggers, and dog walkers. Andrew and Beth made the hike to the park in just under half an hour. But the scenic trail that cut from the park entrance back through the woods to the pond was covered with icy snow, two feet deep in some places. The going was slow.

As they plodded through the crunchy snow, Beth and Andrew could hear the happy shouts and laughter of children bouncing off the trees.

Beth wrapped her gloved hand around Andrew's. "Feels like old times."

"I wonder how many times we've walked this path together," Andrew said.

Beth squeezed his hand. "Who knows? Dozens. Hundreds."

Andrew looked away to hide his stinging eyes. He knew this would be the last time they made this journey together. Lionel's words echoed in his head: *"At 11:58 p.m. Christmas Eve, Beth must keep her date with that speeding taxi. I'm sorry, Andrew, but that is her fate."*

Andrew thought of Bill Murray in *Groundhog Day* and wished he could find a way to freeze this day, to live it over and over again into eternity. He felt Beth watching him.

"Penny for your thoughts," she said.

"You'd be overpaying," Andrew said. How would Beth react if she knew what he was thinking?

"Andrew, are you ashamed of me?"

The question was so abrupt Andrew wasn't sure he heard right. He stopped, and Beth turned to him. "What did you say?"

"Are you ashamed of me?"

The literary agent who prided himself on being able to think on his feet was suddenly tongue-tied. Was she serious? Could she really think that?

He hoped his wife might suddenly crack a smile and let him off the hook, show him she was just pulling his leg. That she knew better. Instead, Beth waited patiently for his answer.

"Beth, how could you think such a thing?"

"I'm not sure why I wonder, but I do," she said. "Back here when we were growing up, I always felt that we had this special connection. I knew that no matter what I did, you were always in my corner cheering me on. But lately, it seems we've lost that. It feels like you've given up on me. And I'm thinking maybe it's because I don't have some big corporate career—"

"Beth, no. That's not . . ." Andrew took her hands in his. "Nothing could be further from the truth. I don't care about all that. I watch you, Beth. I see how you always put others first, how you give of yourself over and over again. Most people wake up in the morning thinking about themselves, how they can further their own ambitions. You wake up thinking about others, how you can make someone's life a little better, a little happier. Beth, you have this . . . this light that flows out of every part of you. I watch you, and I wonder how a person can be so good and caring. And then I wonder how a guy like me could have gotten so lucky as to have someone like Beth McCarthy in his life. Ashamed of you? Are you kidding me, Beth? I don't even deserve you."

Beth smiled. "I love you, Andrew Farmer."

"I love you too." Andrew pulled her in for a kiss.

"Mmm," Beth said. "That's nice. Now, close your eyes."

"Close my eyes?"

"Just close them. I have a surprise for you."

"Oooh, I like the sound of that," Andrew said. He closed his eyes.

"Don't peek," Beth said. Andrew could hear Beth kneel down and scoop up a handful of snow. "Okay, surprise!" She plopped the snow on his head, then burst into a fit of laughter. "Just living in the moment!" she said.

"Oh yeah?" Andrew said. "Now it's *my* moment!"

He grabbed Beth and tackled her to the snowy ground. They wrestled in the snow, laughing and struggling until they finally came to rest with Andrew on top. Beth smiled up at him, brushed a hair back from his face. Andrew caught his breath and gazed down into her lovely flushed face. "I win," he said.

"What's your prize?"

Andrew took her glowing face in his hands, and they melded into a slow, sweet kiss. Afterward, he wiped a bit of ice from her chin with his thumb. "You're my snow angel," he said.

"We haven't kissed like that in a long time," she said. "It felt nice."

Their eyes lingered on each other for a moment, and Andrew wondered if she was trying to read his mind, searching for clues as to the cause of his positive transformation. He was afraid she still didn't trust it, afraid she thought he had some ulterior motive.

"Beth, if you were about to die, would you want to know?"

"What a funny question," she said. "What made you think of that?"

Andrew shrugged. "I don't know. Would you?"

Beth thought for only a moment. "No. I'd want to live whatever time I had left to the fullest, without looking over my shoulder for the Grim Reaper."

Andrew took this in, then nodded. "Me too."

"Help!" A desperate cry shattered their tender moment. "Help!"

It was a young boy's voice, and it was coming from the lake.

Andrew and Beth arrived at the edge of Waller's Pond in less than a minute to find a terrified Tyler standing with a boy and a girl next to a huge snow fort that had just caved in. Beth took the terrified Tyler by the arms.

"Tyler!" she said. "What happened?"

Tyler pointed a trembling finger at the collapsed fort.

"Katie's in there."

Beth and Andrew attacked the frozen pile, digging with their hands, throwing back the packed snow in all directions. "Faster!" Beth said. "There's no time!"

Suddenly a girl's boot emerged from the snowpack. "A foot!" Andrew said. He grabbed it and tried tugging her out, but there was still too much snow weight on top of her.

"Keep digging!" Beth said. They again attacked the pile until the other foot appeared and then a leg. "Okay, pull!" Beth said. They each grabbed a leg and tugged, throwing their collective weight into it. Finally, the boot moved a little, and then a little more until the girl was suddenly pulled free, sending Andrew and Beth tumbling over backward.

Tyler stared wide-eyed at his sister lying cold and still in the snow. Her skin was blue, her eyes shut tight. She wasn't breathing.

"Is she dead?" Tyler said.

Andrew ripped off his coat and draped it over the lifeless girl. Beth began CPR, alternating two breaths with thirty chest compressions. She was calm and collected, totally focused on the task at hand. Andrew pulled out his cell phone and called 911. "Waller's Pond," he said. "Hurry!"

Andrew put an arm around Tyler's shoulders and tried to comfort him. Beyond the snow fort, he noticed a young man sitting on a split-rail fence, watching. He was Asian and in his late teens. He had tattoos on his neck, a nose ring, and several studs piercing his upper and lower lips. He was wearing a black leather jacket and a backward baseball cap.

Odd that he seemed so dispassionate. He hadn't offered to lend a hand and didn't seem the least bit concerned. Then Andrew noticed his earrings. They were gold and dangled in the winter sunlight.

Keys. Lionel's keys.

Andrew gestured to the boy, gave him a "how 'bout a little help?" look, but the boy's gaze remained steady and unblinking. Apparently he had no intention of budging from his perch.

Andrew turned back to the scene at hand as Beth worked furiously to revive the girl. Katie still wasn't moving. Again, Andrew turned to the tattooed stranger. *Please help us*, Andrew thought, and instantly he felt as if the boy had read his thoughts. Still, he made no move to assist.

"When all earthly endeavors have been exhausted, there's always God." As the words danced through Andrew's head in the voice of his grandmother, the boy on the fence cracked the slightest of smiles.

A loud gulp for air brought Andrew back to the moment. Katie coughed three times, then spit up. Tyler shouted, "She's alive!"

Andrew looked back toward the young man on the fence. He was gone.

Beth cradled the stunned girl in her arms. She stroked Katie's hair and soothed her. "It's okay, sweetie. You're okay. Just take it easy."

Katie looked up into Beth's eyes.

"I saw angels," the girl said. "They talked to me. They said they were waiting."

"Waiting for what, sweetie?"

"For you," she said. "The angels are waiting . . . for *you*."

CHAPTER FOURTEEN

*B*eth took a sip of wine. "Some day, huh?"

Andrew and Beth were sitting in a back booth at Mr. Woo's, a favorite local Chinese restaurant on the square. There were candles on the white-clothed tables and a crackling fire in the fireplace. The dining room was tastefully decorated in red, green, and silver. A tiny Christmas tree stood atop an upright piano where a woman sat plunking away the old holiday standards.

By the time the ambulance arrived at Waller's Pond that afternoon, Katie was back to normal and wanted to go home. But Mitch and Megan arrived just after the EMTs and insisted that Katie go to the hospital to be checked out.

Megan called Beth later that afternoon to let her know how grateful they were to them. Katie was doing just fine and showing no ill effects from her near-death experience.

"Can I get you folks anything else?" the waiter said.

"I think we're good," Andrew said. His mouth was dry as melba toast; he felt awkward and out of sorts, like a schoolboy on his first date.

"What is it?" Beth said. "You've hardly said a word since we sat down."

"You were amazing today," Andrew said. "You saved a life. I don't know what I would have done if you hadn't been there."

Beth smiled at him. "You would have saved her."

"I'm not so sure," Andrew said.

Beth put a hand on his arm. "I am." She sat back in her chair, a wistful look on her face. "Weird what Katie said, wasn't it?"

"What do you mean?" Andrew said. He knew exactly what she meant.

"You know. 'The angels are waiting for you.' Waiting for *me*. Didn't you find that a little strange?"

"Oh, well, she was delirious," he said. He signaled the waiter for the check. He wanted to get off this track as quickly as possible.

"I don't know," Beth said. "I've read about near-death experiences. Lots of people have had them. Maybe she was bringing me a message from the other side."

Andrew laughed nervously. "The other side?"

"You know, the spirit world. I just think what she said was interesting, that's all. I happen to believe we have a spiritual self—our real and true self. It's just hidden most of the time."

"Well, how do we get it to show itself?" Andrew tried his best to sound sincere.

"Love," Beth said. "Whenever we love unselfishly, our true and perfect self shines through."

"I believe that," Andrew said.

"Oh really?" Beth said. "Honey, no offense—it's just that I've never known you to be a metaphysical kind of guy."

"Well, I've changed."

"Oh?" Beth said. She took a sip of water. "Since when?"

"Since . . ." Andrew glanced over just as the piano player blew him a kiss. She had stopped playing and was looking right at him. He nearly knocked over his wineglass. "Oops."

Beth smiled as if she found his boyish awkwardness endearing. "You'd better slow down, mister. Or I may have to cut you off."

"Uh, sorry," Andrew said. "I guess the piano player's going on break."

"What piano player?"

Andrew looked back at the piano. It was gone, and so was the woman. "I . . . uh . . . I was just . . . making a joke," he said.

"Okay," Beth said. "Why are you so jumpy tonight?"

"I'm not jumpy. I'm . . . excited. Very excited."

"Why?"

Andrew reached beneath the table and pulled out a large gift-wrapped parcel.

Beth smiled. "Oh, right. The mystery package you've been carrying around that I'm not supposed to ask about."

"That's the one," Andrew said. He placed it in front of her.

Beth rubbed her hands together. "For me?"

Andrew nodded.

"Oh, goody. I love surprises," she said.

"So I've heard."

"I can't believe you got this for me," Beth said.

"Beth, you don't even know what it is yet."

"I know, but I still can't believe it."

"Just open it!"

Beth carefully peeled away the wrapping paper and lifted the top off the box. She gasped and put a hand to her mouth. It was the old music box, the one she'd fallen in love with at the Forever Christmas store.

"Oh, Andrew," she said.

She cranked the little wind-up key and stared dreamily as the miniature skaters came to life and started weaving their way across the tiny frozen pond. She leaned across the table and gave Andrew a kiss. "I love it. Thank you."

Andrew felt a rush of pleasure. Lionel told him he needed to get Beth a farewell Christmas gift, and it looked like he'd nailed it the first time out of the gate. It was almost too easy.

"Guess we should get the check," he said. He again tried to signal the waiter, then noticed that Beth was staring at him, a half smile on her lips. "What?" he said.

"I was just thinking about Katie and Tyler and how cute they are."

"Yes," Andrew said. "They're cute kids."

"Does it ever make you want one?" Beth said. "Or two?"

Andrew could feel her watching his face for a reaction. He thought about faking it, about putting on a show, but he knew he wasn't that good of an actor. Beth would know he wasn't being sincere, and it would only make things worse.

"Beth, I just——" He searched desperately for the right words. Why now? Why did she have to bring this up now? In the history of timing, this had to be the absolute worst. "I just don't think that *now* is the right time," he said. The moment the words left his lips, he knew they were lame and weak and pathetic.

Beth nodded and carefully dabbed her lips with her napkin. Andrew could see she was struggling to keep the tears at bay.

"Andrew, I know we've talked about waiting for the perfect time, but I'm not getting any younger, and it just seems that maybe *now's* as perfect as it's ever going to get."

Andrew felt the knot tighten in his stomach. "Listen, Beth..."

"Never mind." She dropped her napkin and pushed back from the table. "Forget I brought it up. I have to go to the ladies' room."

She started off and then abruptly turned back. "Andrew, when we were younger, you used to tell me you couldn't wait to start a family. Somewhere along the way, I guess you changed your mind."

Andrew watched her walk away and knew she didn't want him to see her cry. He felt a lump in his throat. No matter how hard he'd tried to make the perfect weekend, reality kept rearing its ugly mug to burst the balloon.

"*Bravo!*"

Andrew turned to see the piano lady sitting in Beth's seat. She was an attractive woman in her midthirties with raven hair and an olive complexion. Her lips were bright red and her cheeks dusted with blush. He immediately noticed her necklace. A large gold key, dangling there like a heavenly calling card.

"You have outdone yourself, my friend," the piano player said.

Andrew was in no mood to be hospitable. "Seat's taken."

"Not for much longer." Her tone held a touch of mockery that made Andrew want to toss his half-empty bowl of dim sum at her. "Look, lady—"

"Isabelle," the piano player said.

"Isabelle. If you're not here to help out, I'd appreciate it if you'd just leave me alone. I don't need another reminder about the ticking clock. I can tell time."

Isabelle threw back her head and laughed. "Very funny. Now, tell me, funny man, why don't you want kids?"

Andrew glared a hole through her. "I *do* want to have kids! More than anything."

The woman gave him a dubious look. "That's not what you said when Beth brought up the subject. You said, and I quote: 'I just don't think that now is the right time.' Unquote."

"I'm an idiot. Okay?" Andrew said. "There, I said it. You happy now?" Andrew noticed that a few of the customers were watching him.

"You do know they can't see me, right?" Isabelle said.

Andrew turned beet red and lowered his voice. "I've had the wrong priorities. I've been caught up in my career."

The piano lady winked at him. "That's the first smart thing I've heard you say since I met you. But being an idiot with wrong priorities is just part of your problem. What about your father?"

"My father?" Andrew said. "What does he have to do with whether I want kids?"

"More than you think."

"What do you mean?"

"You just don't get it," she said. "All of our thoughts and feelings are connected. Each one affects the other. Maybe your attitude toward your father has influenced your desire to become a father."

"You sound more like a shrink than an angel," Andrew said.

"Oh no," Isabelle said. "A shrink will tell you it's not your fault. We angels know better. The universe is harmonic, Andrew. If your life isn't harmonious, it's because you've chosen disharmony. Believe it or not, you've chosen your present situation. You're the reason I'm here, and you're the reason you will lose the best thing that ever happened to you tomorrow night at 11:58 p.m."

Andrew felt his temperature rising. "You're crazy. Nobody would choose this."

Isabelle put a hand on his arm. "Deal with your father, Andrew."

"If I deal with my father, will that help me with Beth?"

"Only those who forgive earn the right to be forgiven," the woman said.

"Where'd you learn that—angel boot camp?"

She picked a fortune cookie from Beth's plate and handed it to Andrew. He cracked open the brittle cookie and pulled out the little slip of paper. "Only those who forgive earn the right to be forgiven."

"Forgive my father? You have no idea what he—"

"I know more than you, Andrew."

"Okay. Well, pretend you're not an angel for a minute," he said. "Pretend you're just a fallible old mortal like me. Would you forgive him if your father did that to your mother?"

"I've forgiven a lot worse," Isabelle said.

"Well, what if I don't think it's right? What if I think it would be disloyal to my mother's memory if I just forgive and forget?"

"Andrew, Andrew. You are such a naïve boy. Your mother has long ago forgiven your father. If you really want to pay tribute to her memory, you need to do the same."

"What do you know about my mother?" Andrew said.

Isabelle gave him a look.

"I get it . . . you're an *angel*," he said.

She winked at him. "Now you're catching on."

Andrew took a gulp of water. "So, what about my gift? Beth loved it."

"Very nice, Andrew." She appraised the music box. "Nice, but not quite right."

"What do you mean, not right?" Andrew said. "You—well, Lionel—said to get a Christmas present, and I got a Christmas present. I'm not sure what you want from me."

Isabelle looked over to see Beth returning from the bathroom. "Here she comes. Remember. Go see your dad."

The walk back to the inn was awkward and silent. Andrew toted the oversized music box that now seemed a wasted effort. Beth walked slowly, her hands in her coat pockets. She seemed lost in thought and in no mood for conversation. Andrew decided it was best to give her space.

A few blocks away, the church bell from River Falls Christian started to peal, reminding Andrew once again that time was marching after him. He looked at Beth. He hated the feeling of being cut off from her.

He decided to play his only card. "Let's go see my dad."

Beth stopped in her tracks, faced him. "Andrew, are you serious?"

"Yes. The nursing home is only a few blocks from here. I bet he's still up."

Ten minutes later they were standing outside the Shady Tree Nursing Home.

"What changed your mind?" Beth said.

"I don't know," Andrew said. "I was just thinking that all the resentment I've built up over the years for my father can't be good for me. And maybe it's time I tried to, you know, deal with my . . . feelings and stuff."

Beth gave him a curious look. "Andrew, that's very self-aware of you. That's not like you."

"Thanks."

"You know what I mean. You've never been one to self-examine."

"Yeah," Andrew said. "I know. It's just . . . I don't want to let anything come between you and me. Not anymore."

Beth smiled and took his hand. "Come on, then. Let's go say hello."

The moment they entered the nursing home recreation room, they spotted Henry Farmer sitting alone at a card table, aimlessly shuffling a deck of cards. Andrew thought how small and frail his father looked. There was an oxygen tank next to him, a bottle of pills on the table.

"Heard I could find a game of gin rummy here," Beth said.

Henry looked up. At first he seemed confused, then he spotted her and smiled. "Beth?" he said. "Is it really you?"

Andrew hung back, let Beth take the lead. He further appraised his dad. The years on the road, the cigarettes and endless drinking, had taken their toll. If Beth felt the same, she didn't let on. She gave Henry a kiss on the forehead, and he flushed bright pink.

"Well, if this don't beat all," Henry said. "If I'd have known you were coming, I'd have baked a cake."

Beth took the chair across from him. "We wanted to surprise you. Besides, I'm trying to cut back on sweets."

Henry laughed. "I don't know why. You're still quite the dish."

"Oh, stop it," Beth said. "You'll make me blush."

Henry took a quick hit of oxygen as Andrew looked away.

Beth caught his eye, gave him a coaxing look, and mouthed the words, "Say something."

"How are ya?" Andrew said. It came out stiff and forced. He felt his stomach tighten, his pulse quicken. The old resentments started to simmer; he wanted to turn and run out of the room. What was he thinking, coming here? He wasn't ready for this.

"I'm old, that's how I am," Henry said. "I have to tote this blasted tank with me everywhere I go, but other than that, I guess I can't complain." He gave a wheezing chuckle. "But sometimes I still do."

The old man winked at Beth, then sized up his son. "You look good. A little thicker, maybe. Must be Beth's good cooking."

"It's been awhile," Andrew said.

After a tense moment, Beth stepped in to move things along. "So, merry Christmas!"

"Same to you, sweetheart," Henry said. "C'mon. Tell me everything. You know how I love the gossip."

"Well, let's see . . . ," Beth said. "We just came down for the weekend—sort of a spur-of-the-moment decision. Right, Andrew?"

"Yep," Andrew said. He couldn't seem to force himself to meet his father's eye.

"River Falls is so beautiful in the winter," Beth said. "Magical."

"That it is," Henry said. "Don't get out much to enjoy it anymore, though. Funny, isn't it? All my traveling, all the places I've been, and I end up back here in the end. Good old River Falls."

Andrew couldn't let this pass. "A little late, don't you think?" Henry looked up. "Mom's long dead, your home sold and gone, and now you come back to settle down. Nice timing."

Henry shook his head. "So that's why you're here? To make me feel guilty?"

"No," Beth said. She put a restraining hand on Andrew's arm.

Andrew seethed. How dare he? "Guilty?" he said. "I'm surprised you know the meaning of the word."

"Well, merry Christmas to you too," Henry said.

Beth gave Andrew a pleading look. "Please. Not now." She turned back to the old man, took his frail hand. "We're not here to talk about the past. We just wanted to say hello and see how you're doing."

Henry relaxed a little, gave Andrew a half smile. "Beth keeps me posted through her letters. Looks like you've made it big. Living the dream."

"I do okay," Andrew said.

"Okay?" Henry said. "Sounds to me like you're a real big shot. Six-figure job, fancy apartment, expense account. Isn't that a kick? You turned out to be a salesman, just like your old man. Guess the apple didn't fall far from the tree."

Andrew had heard enough. "How dare you take credit for my success! You have nothing to do with who I am! I made it in spite of you, not because of you."

"Andrew." Beth tried to cut in, but he ignored her.

He fixed his father with a cold stare. "You have some nerve."

"Now, hold on, son," Henry said. "I never said I—"

"Don't call me son! I'm your *offspring*, not your son. A son is someone you're there for, someone you care about. I don't think I qualify."

"Andrew, please," Beth said. She was almost in tears. "Please don't do this."

"Look, Andy," Henry said. "I know I wasn't there for you as much as I shoulda been, but my business required me to travel . . ."

"Your business, or your *girlfriends*?" Andrew said.

"I worked hard for my family! I kept food on the table. You and your mother never wanted for anything."

"Except for *one* thing," Andrew said.

Then he turned and walked out, leaving Beth and Henry alone.

Outside the nursing home, Andrew paced and tried to get ahold on his tempestuous swirl of emotions. He kicked at the snow. His father hadn't been there when he needed him, and now here he was at the worst possible moment. Andrew could imagine Beth back inside, consoling the old man, apologizing for his rude and unforgiving son. She'd find a way to make him feel better. That was Beth.

"Andrew."

Andrew looked up to see Beth standing there, watching him. The look on her face told him he'd not only hurt his father by his outburst, he'd hurt her too.

"I'm sorry, Beth. The way I was in there . . . it's inexcusable. I guess it was a mistake coming here." Andrew shoved his hands in his coat pockets and shook his head. He was lost. He thought he could handle it, thought he could control his emotions for Beth's sake, and he had failed miserably.

"No, it's my fault," Beth said. "I should have told you he was here, that I was in touch with him."

Andrew took her in his arms and thought again about spilling his terrible secret. If there was a chance she'd believe him, one chance in a million, it might help save her life. He must tell her, even if she thought he was crazy as a loon; he had to try. Then her words flashed through his mind.

"I'd want to live whatever time I had left to the fullest, without looking over my shoulder for the Grim Reaper."

Beth took his face in her hands and looked him right in the eyes. "Andrew, did you see? Did you see how proud he is of you?"

Andrew swallowed and looked away. "Beth, I'll deal with my father later. I promise. Just not now. Not tonight."

Tears welled up in Andrew's eyes, and when one rolled down his frozen cheek, Beth wiped it away with the tip of her gloved thumb. Andrew Farmer never cried. Never. She kissed one of his cheeks, then the other. "Hey," she said. "It's okay. Everything is going to be all right."

But Andrew knew there was another issue left on the table. "Beth, I think that the reason I'm reluctant to have kids is because I'm afraid I won't be a good father. What if bad parenting is hereditary?"

Beth wrapped her arms around him. "Oh, Andrew. You'll be a wonderful father. Of that I have no doubt."

"Beth, I—"

"Shhh," Beth said. She put her index finger to his lips. "We don't have to know all the answers tonight."

She buried her head in his chest as Andrew looked up at the snowflakes swirling in the streetlamp and whispered to the wind, "I need more time. Please. I just need a little more time."

CHAPTER FIFTEEN

On the way back to the inn, Andrew and Beth cut through the nearly deserted downtown. The moonlight reflecting off the snow gave the night a hauntingly bluish tint. Andrew looked up at a winter night sky thick with stars. "Wow," he said. "Would you look at that?" Beth followed his gaze.

"Yeah. God's masterpiece," she said. She stole a look at her husband. "I really like this version of Andy Farmer."

Andrew smiled. "Andy Farmer 2.0."

Beth squeezed his arm. "I should have upgraded years ago."

As they rounded a corner, the sound of music drifted across the tranquil square. "Listen," Andrew said. "Hear it?"

"Hear what?" Beth said.

Andrew pulled her along with him. "C'mon!"

"Wait! Where are we—?"

Andrew pulled Beth over to the lighted storefront of Antoine's Italian Restaurant. Through the picture frame window, Beth and Andrew watched young newlyweds slowly shuffle cheek to cheek across a makeshift dance floor to the music of a wedding band. The bride wore a tastefully old-fashioned wedding dress, and the groom was in tails. The dancing couple gazed lovingly into each other's eyes as family and friends looked on.

Beth smiled. "It's their first dance."

Andrew looked at his wife. "Beth, would you do it all over again?"

"Do what over again?"

"Marry me?"

Beth looked into his eyes, and Andrew wasn't sure what her answer would be. He wished he could reach out and snatch the question back. What if she said—

"Of course I would," Beth said. "You're the best thing that ever happened to me." Andrew smiled, and for a moment all his cares and fears faded into the background of the frosty winter night. The female lead singer's voice was rich and sweet as it carried out into the vacant square.

It could have been the steeple bell
That wrapped us up in its spell.
It only took one kiss to know
It must have been the mistletoe.

"Remember our first dance?" Beth said.

"It was to 'Unforgettable,'" Andrew said. He took Beth's hand in his, slipped his other hand down around her waist, and they started to slowly move to the music. They swayed back and forth in the cold night air, dancing in rhythm with the newlyweds, lost in each other's arms, as the singer continued her soulful song:

On Christmas Eve our wish came true
That I would fall in love with you.
It only took one kiss to know
It must have been the mistletoe.

Back at the River Falls Inn, Andrew sat on the edge of the bed staring at Beth as she waged a losing battle with sleep. He marveled at how utterly beautiful she looked, kissed by the soft moonlight that spilled through the hotel room window. He wanted her to stay awake, to keep talking to him, but as her words grew more and more slurred, he knew he'd soon be alone again with his thoughts.

Andrew glanced at the digital clock on the nightstand: 11:51.

"What were you saying?" she said. She could no longer keep her eyes open.

"I was remembering the time you went out with Duffy Waldrop just to make me jealous," Andrew said.

Beth mumbled, "No, I didn't. I actually *liked* Duffy. Sort of, anyway." She patted the mattress. "Now, come to bed, Duffy."

"Ha-ha," Andrew said. "I will soon. I just want to stare at you a little while longer."

Beth mumbled, her words swallowed in sleep, "Weirdo."

Andrew chuckled. He'd never felt so alive in his life. He just wanted to drink her in, to savor every moment of her existence. A tear rolled down his cheek, and he quickly wiped it away with his sleeve. No time for tears. He had to hold it together.

Beth had fallen silent; she was breathing in the soft rhythms of sleep. Andrew sensed something—a strange tingling, some sort of magical tug that drew him to the room window. He pulled back the curtain and looked out. Down below, beneath a streetlamp, Lionel waited for him.

"What do you want?" Andrew didn't even attempt to hide his irritation. He pulled his overcoat snugly around his pajamas.

"Nice to see you too, Andrew," Lionel said. "Notice the time?"

"Yeah, I know. Eleven fifty-eight."

"On the dot," Lionel said. "Exactly twenty-four hours to go."

"Think again," Andrew said. "I don't care who you are or who sent you. There's no way I let Beth anywhere near that street tomorrow night!"

"Now, Andrew, I told you—"

"I won't let her die! Understand? Banish me to hell, turn me into a zombie. I really don't care anymore!"

Lionel chuckled. "A zombie? C'mon, Andrew. We have a deal."

"Well, the deal's off!" Andrew said.

"Sorry, Andrew. It's not your call."

"Then let's renegotiate," Andrew said.

"The terms are final."

"Oh yeah?" Andrew said. "Says who?"

Lionel glanced up at the sky. "A much bigger power than either you or me."

Andrew jabbed a finger at Lionel's chest. "I thought angels were supposed to help people, not kill them."

"Andrew, don't do this. Accept what's to come. It's her time."

"No! I won't accept it! Change her time! Change her fate! Don't angels have powers?"

"Andrew, we've been over this. We have an agreement."

"I never signed anything."

"A binding verbal agreement," Lionel said. "Now, your energies would be better spent looking for Beth's last Christmas gift."

"I don't care about a stupid gift! I want my wife."

"If Beth skips her date with destiny, the cosmic balance will be thrown out of whack. My boss won't let that happen."

Andrew looked Lionel in the eye. His bravado was gone. He was just plain scared. "Please, Lionel. There's got to be a loophole. There's *always* a loophole."

Lionel considered this for several seconds.

"Andrew, if you truly love her, you'll figure it out." He turned and strolled off down the sidewalk.

Andrew breathed a desperate sigh as the church bell began to toll midnight and the locksmith angel gradually faded away into the bitter night air.

"No peeking, Mr. Farmer!" Christmas Eve morning, the last day of Beth's life, found Andrew and Beth standing in front of the big Fraser fir tree in River Falls Town Square. They each held an inscribed metallic Christmas ornament. Her green one said "Beth," his red one said "Andrew."

Andrew teased her. "Now, why do we have to close our eyes again?"

"Because I say so," Beth said. "We can't just plunk our ornaments on any old branch. We have to feel it. *Feel* the tree."

Andrew reached out and rubbed a branch. Beth gave him a playful punch in the arm. "No! I don't mean *literally*. You have to feel it in your heart. Then you'll know just the right spot for your ornament."

Andrew grinned. "Oh. Got it."

"All right," Beth said. "Close your eyes." Andrew obeyed. "Now concentrate, and let all the stress flow out of you. Think of the tree, only the tree. *Be* the tree. Then, when you're ready, find the perfect spot for your ornament."

Andrew cracked one eyelid and spied on Beth; she had her eyes dutifully clenched shut as she reached out, blindly searching for the perfect branch. Once he saw where she placed her green ornament, he placed his red one right next to it.

"Okay," Beth said. "Now you can open your eyes."

They opened their eyes and saw their two matching ornaments dangling side by side. "Perfect," she said. "Even though I know you peeked." She gave him a quick peck on the cheek. "Okay, let's go home!" She grabbed Andrew's arm, started pulling him along with her.

"Home? Beth, no!" Andrew dug in his heels and stopped her in her tracks.

She gave him a puzzled look. "No?" she said.

"I mean, I think we should stay awhile longer," Andrew said. "Don't you like being here? I love being here. Let's spend Christmas in River Falls."

"What?" Beth said. "I thought you didn't like River Falls. 'A trip to the library's bigger than this.' Remember?"

"Well, I've changed my mind," Andrew said. "We can hang out with Mitch, Megan, and the kids. Maybe you can save Katie's life again."

"Andrew . . ."

"Beth, please say yes! It'll feel like a real family Christmas."

Beth smiled, pulled him in close, and whispered, "Uh-uh. I want to spend Christmas in Manhattan with you. Just the two of us, snuggled up by the fire in our cozy apartment in front of the Christmas tree. Which we still have to get, by the way."

"But—"

Beth silenced him with a kiss. "No argument. You said it was my choice. Remember? And I choose home for Christmas."

Andrew could scarcely concentrate as he paid the hotel bill. He was barely conscious of Mr. Gibbons behind the counter. The innkeeper was talking about the weather and holiday traffic, his aching feet. To Andrew, it was all just background clatter. His mind was on the wall clock behind the desk. Each tick sounded like a crashing cymbal.

"Your wife not going with you?" Mr. Gibbons said.

Andrew looked up at him. He was vaguely aware the man had aimed a question in his direction. Old Gibbons was happy to repeat it. "I said, your wife not going with you? I was being funny. I'm quick with the jokes."

"I wish she weren't," Andrew said.

Gibbons cocked his ear at him. "What's that you say?"

Andrew raised his voice a few decibels. "She's still packing." He noticed the time on the wall clock: 9:58 a.m.

Gibbons noticed Andrew's clock watching. "Clock's a few minutes slow," he said. Andrew shot him a scathing look, and the innkeeper smiled. "Wouldn't want you to miss your train." Gibbons handed Andrew his credit card receipt. "If you'll just give me your John Hancock." Andrew hurriedly signed his name as the squeaky front door opened.

"Good morning, Mr. Whitman," Gibbons said. "How was your walk?"

"Fine," a man's voice said from behind Andrew.

Andrew wheeled about to see his most famous literary client standing just inside the door, kicking the snow from his boots. Alistair Whitman was a barrel of a man with a thick grayish beard and a shock of frazzled white hair. His voice was commanding, and his words came out as if each syllable were gold. The renowned writer had a look of amusement on his face when he saw his agent.

"Well, if it isn't Andrew Farmer."

"Alistair?"

"Oh, so you two know each other," Gibbons said.

Whitman and Andrew ignored the innkeeper and shook hands. "And here I thought you hated this place," Whitman said.

Andrew gaped at him. "Alistair, what are you doing here?"

"What am I doing here? What do you think? Working on the sequel. Andrew, it was your idea, remember?" Whitman looked at the innkeeper. "Go back to River Falls and get inspired, he tells me."

Andrew couldn't remember the first thing about any such conversation, but then, he was a mite preoccupied. "Oh, right," he said. "Sorry. I've been a bit scatterbrained lately."

Whitman smiled. "So I hear congratulations are in order."

Andrew gave him a puzzled look. "Congratulations?"

"I hear old man Townsend's dispatching you to the left coast to launch the new LA office." Whitman looked at Gibbons. "People just can't seem to get enough of those frightful celebrity tell-all books. Andrew, you should fit right in out there with those Hollywood sharks. Just don't forget about your favorite client."

Andrew wanted to turn and run out the door. This was the last conversation on earth he wanted to be having at that moment.

"Nothing's set in stone yet . . . ," Andrew said.

"Oh?" Whitman said. "That's not what I heard. I heard it was a done deal. Be sure to take plenty of sunscreen."

Andrew noticed that the author was no longer looking at him. His eyes were now locked on the top of the lobby staircase. Andrew followed his gaze, and his heart stopped. Beth was looking down at him, her hang-up bag slung over her shoulder. For a brief moment, he wasn't sure she'd overheard their conversation, and then he saw it in her eyes—a mixture of shock and pain. She'd heard, all right. She'd heard everything.

"Beth . . . ?"

Beth hurried down the stairs without a word, shoved off Andrew's attempt to restrain her, and was out the lobby door in a flash. Andrew froze, stared from Whitman to Gibbons and back again, and then bolted after her.

"Beth, wait!" Andrew hit a patch of ice on the front walk as he tried to catch up to his fleeing wife. He lost his balance, and his feet went flying out from beneath him. He landed hard on his back, the cold cement punching the breath out of him. He lay on the ground for a moment, gasping for air. By the time he was able to suck in enough oxygen to get up, Beth was already in the back-seat of Larry's cab. Andrew grabbed the door before she could close it. "Beth, please! I was going to tell you just as soon—"

Beth glared up at him from the backseat. "When, Andrew? When the moving van arrived?"

"Beth, I'm sorry. I should have—"

"Andrew, how could you do this? We're a couple. We're sup-posed to plan our lives together."

"Beth, I know. I just wanted to surprise you . . ."

"Surprise me? Well, you succeeded. I'm surprised. Tell me, Andrew, what were you thinking?"

"I don't know. That it was an amazing opportunity, maybe a full partnership at double the salary, a share of the profits, and no more New York winters."

"I love those winters, Andrew. And I love our life in New York. Did you ever for one second—when you were dreaming about your big salary and share of the profits—think about your wife? What I might want? Did you, Andrew? Even for a moment?"

Andrew slowly shook his head. He couldn't lie to her. Not now. He had only thought of himself, his career, his status. His wife had been an afterthought.

"No," he said. "I didn't."

Beth's face changed. The anger was gone. There was only pain. He had broken the heart of his best friend, the love of his life. He'd lost her. The game was over.

Beth pulled the car door out of his grip and slammed it shut. "Train station, Larry," she said.

Andrew watched as the taxi pulled away, stunned and confused and out of ideas. As he stood there in the cold, a light snow began to fall.

What had he done? Was this the last time he'd ever see her alive? He had thrown away the best gift God had ever given him. He had taken Beth for granted, and the bill had come due. He was going to lose her, and he knew he was getting exactly what he deserved.

In a flash, his life with Beth flickered through his mind like a movie trailer. He saw them as children splashing in a backyard kiddie pool, sharing an awkward first kiss at a friend's birthday party. Then a foggy memory of Beth by his dying mother's bedside, holding Emma's frail, quivering hand, whispering words of comfort. He saw his young bride's joyous tearstained face as he lifted her veil on their wedding day.

The scenes whisked by on fast-forward, moving so quickly he could barely make them out. Then there she was again, standing in the window of their apartment, solemnly decorating the tree as Andrew waited for the cab that would take him away from her.

Only this time, she turned and looked down at him, a wounded expression on her face. She mouthed words that were easy to read. "Good-bye, Andrew. I'll miss you."

Last of all, he flashed back to the snow-laden New York street on that terrible night. The relentless taxi bearing down on Beth, kicking up a spray of soft white powder in its wake. He saw himself watching, helpless and hopeless and terrified, unable to move, unable to save her. He closed his eyes as if to shut out the awful scene, but try as he might, he couldn't look away. He had to watch.

The whistle of an approaching train stirred him from his fatalistic thoughts. The visions vanished. He glanced around, refocused as the whistle sounded again. The train was arriving at River Falls Station.

Beth's train.

Andrew felt a sudden surge of adrenaline. It was the fourth quarter, and he was far behind, but the game wasn't over yet. Maybe he would fail at Lionel's assignment; maybe he was about to lose his wife. But he hadn't yet. He still had more than thirteen hours to go.

Andrew cupped his hands and shouted at the top of his lungs, "Lionel! Where are you? Show yourself!" He turned to see old Gibbons watching him from the inn porch.

"I need a ride!" Andrew yelled. "Now!"

The cold engine of Gibbons's old pickup sputtered and coughed as he tried to crank it to life. "C'mon, Bessie, you can do it."

"Please hurry!" Andrew said. He checked his watch.

Gibbons tried the key again. "The old girl can be a bit ornery at times," he said. The engine clicked and thumped. "Nope. She's not ready yet."

Andrew had waited long enough. "Forget it!" he said. He shoved open the truck door and made a run for it.

CHAPTER SIXTEEN

You just missed her." A smiling porter greeted Andrew as he ran from the terminal out onto the train platform. For a moment, he wasn't sure if the porter meant Beth or the train. Out of breath from his mad dash through the icy streets, Andrew doubled over and sucked in air.

When he looked down the tracks, he could see the 10:35 a.m. train to New York growing smaller as it left River Falls. Andrew slumped down on a bench. How could he have let this happen? The porter felt a wave of pity for the man. "Be another at one thirty," he said.

Andrew stared up at him. The porter was tall and lean, with a perfectly groomed handlebar mustache that made him look as if he'd stepped through a wormhole from an old western town. His neat red-and-black-trimmed uniform had shiny, freshly polished brass buttons. His hat was fire-engine red with a dark brown bill; the gold chain of a watch dangled from his pocket. The metal name tag on his breast simply said "Porter." Whether it was his name or his occupation, Andrew couldn't fathom.

"I can't wait that long," Andrew said. "Is there a car rental place around here?"

The porter chuckled. "Car rental? In River Falls? No, sir. 'Fraid not."

"Of course not," Andrew said. He whipped out his wallet. "What about you? Do you have a car I could rent . . . or buy?" Andrew held up a wad of bills. "I have cash."

"Mister, all I got's an old jalopy, and she's not for sale."

Andrew grew more desperate. If this guy wanted to barter, he'd come to the right place. "Name your price!" Andrew peeled out three crisp hundred-dollar bills. "How about I rent it for three hundred and return it tomorrow with a full tank of gas."

The porter grinned. "Sir . . ."

"You can trust me! Here, I'll leave you my credit cards." Andrew started to empty the contents of his wallet. The kindly porter raised a hand.

"Sir, even if I was willing to lend you my car, it wouldn't make a difference. With the holiday traffic as bad as it is, it would make more sense to wait for the one thirty. The turnpike's a parking lot all the way to Meadville. Train'll get you home a whole lot quicker."

Andrew nodded. "Thanks." As he started to turn away, Andrew saw the porter lift a gold watch from his pocket and pop it open. Dangling from the chain was a fob—a large, fancy gold key.

A steady snow sifted down on River Falls as Andrew trudged through the square, his hands in his coat pockets and his eyes on the ground. He wasn't sure where he was headed or why. He just knew he couldn't sit still.

He passed the Forever Christmas store and cut across the square to the big fir tree where he found the twin ornaments he and Beth had placed that morning. A new wave of hopelessness washed over him. Here he was, trapped in his hometown, and Beth was moving farther and farther away from him by the moment. He took out his phone, checked to see if she'd texted him back. Nothing.

She wouldn't answer. She'd given up on him, on them.

Andrew felt his phone vibrate in his pocket and quickly checked for a text from Beth. But instead of Beth on his phone screen, he saw Lionel's smiling face. The text read simply, *Forgiveness is divine.*

Andrew deleted the message. When he looked up from his phone, he was no longer by the Christmas tree. He was standing in front of the Shady Tree Nursing Home.

Andrew found his father in the Shady Tree rec room sitting at his usual card table. Henry Farmer was all alone, save for an ancient woman in a wheelchair who had fallen asleep in front of the television. Andrew watched his old man shuffle the deck twice, then start laying out the cards for a game of solitaire. Halfway through the dealing, he paused to take a hit of oxygen. When he turned back to his cards, Andrew was standing there in front of the table.

"Hey, Dad."

"Andrew?" Henry looked past him, searching for Beth.

"Just me," Andrew said. "Mind if I sit down?"

"Pull up a stump," Henry said.

Andrew took a seat across from his father. He sighed deeply as he gathered his thoughts. Where to begin?

"Dad, I was wrong. I never should have said those things to you. I'm sorry."

A narrow smile creased the old man's lips. "No apology needed, son. I don't blame you one bit. I'm the one who owes you an apology. As a matter of fact, I've been thinking about it all morning. I heard this quote the other day: 'There are three stages of a man's life. He believes in Santa Claus; he doesn't believe in Santa Claus; he *is* Santa Claus.' When it came to my family, I skipped the last stage—and, for that, I'm truly sorry. Andy, I know I wasn't there for you. I think about it all the time, and I'd give anything for a chance to do it over again, to make things right. Unfortunately, God doesn't hand out do-overs."

Andrew gave a grim smile. If only he knew.

"I can't change the past," Henry said. "I just hope and pray there's still time, that I can be in your life somehow. Even if just a little."

Andrew looked at his father. So this was what forgiveness felt like. Not too shabby. He put a hand on Henry's arm.

"I'm pretty big on second chances right now."

Henry smiled to stifle his tears. Then he winked at his son. "So how about a game of pinochle?"

"Dad, I'd like to. I really would. But I have to find Beth."

"Find Beth?"

"I messed up. I messed up bad. I really let her down, and now I think I've lost her."

Henry nodded as if he understood perfectly. "You're lucky, Andrew. All the years I spent running around, all the years out on the road, I didn't realize how much I loved your mother until it was too late. She was gone, and I never got the chance to tell her how lucky I was to have someone as wonderful as her. It's not too late for you, Andrew. You have time. You'll find Beth, and you'll make things right. She'll understand. The two of you will have a lifetime of happiness together."

The irony of his father's words seared Andrew's soul. That lifetime of happiness was quickly slipping through his fingers. His brokenhearted wife was miles and miles away.

And the clock was ticking.

CHAPTER SEVENTEEN

To Andrew, the two-and-a-half-hour train ride from River Falls to Penn Station seemed like an eternity. The train was packed with holiday travelers, weary parents letting their sugar-rushed kids run rampant from one car to another. Andrew spent the first hour trying in vain to reach Beth by phone until his cell died somewhere in western New Jersey.

When the doors opened at Penn Station, the train was half an hour late. Andrew bolted like a caged animal. He dodged and darted his way through the mob and bounded up the exit stairs to 34th Street. It was already nearly dark; the steady snow of the arriving storm fell on a city glowing with red and green and all things Christmas. The massive tree of lights outside Macy's cast an amber glow on the hundreds of faces waiting in line for one last shot on Santa's lap.

Andrew darted out into the street and started wildly flagging passing cabs. Occupied. Out of service. Suddenly, he saw one pull up in front of Macy's. As a family of four piled out of the backseat, Andrew made a dash for it, barely outrunning a skateboard-toting teenage boy in a hoodie sweatshirt. Andrew jumped in back and closed the door.

"Carnegie Hill. And please hurry!"

But there was no hurrying on this snowy Christmas Eve in New York City. The unusually heavy holiday traffic crawled along at a snail's pace, and not even a skilled New York cabbie could find an opening.

At 52nd and Broadway, Andrew decided he'd had enough. He tossed a crumpled twenty in the front seat and jumped out, intercepting an empty bike taxi that was easily darting in and around the traffic logjam, heading in the opposite direction.

Andrew darted in front of the bicyclist, cutting him off. "Hey, buddy! I need to go to Carnegie Hill!"

The driver maneuvered around him, kept pedaling. "Not with me, you ain't," he said.

"How about for a hundred bucks?" The driver slammed on his brakes.

Fifteen minutes later and a hundred dollars lighter, Andrew stood at the front door of his apartment building. He put his old key in the lock without a second thought. *Click.* It turned with no problem. He shoved open the door and hurried inside.

"Beth!" Andrew raced through the apartment room to room. "Beth?"

Empty. In the bedroom, his eyes lighted on the digital clock on the bedside table: 4:58 p.m.

Seven hours to go.

The winter storm arrived full force as Andrew desperately searched their Upper East Side neighborhood. He checked every spot he could think of where Beth might be: the flower shop, the bookstore, the corner grocer. Nobody had seen her, and most merchants were preparing to close up shop and head home to their families. Where would Beth go? What would she be doing? Andrew's mind tripped over itself as he tried to pluck a single right idea out of his rush of frantic thoughts.

He looked up into the falling snow. "Beth. Where are you?"

All of a sudden he saw her, just across the street. She stood at a storefront window, watching an electric train putter around a winding train track.

Andrew heaved a sigh of relief. He walked across the street and gently touched her on the shoulder. "Beth?"

Startled, she turned to him. Not Beth. The young woman with Beth's height and hair gave him an annoyed look and hurried on up the sidewalk.

"So sorry," Andrew said. "I thought you were . . ."

The woman didn't look back to acknowledge his awkward apology—she just kept going and disappeared around the corner.

Andrew's heart sank. The clock was ticking ever closer to zero hour, and his wife was lost somewhere in a snowy white sea of eight million souls. Again he looked up at the sky. He closed his eyes and let the wet snow melt against his skin.

"Show me the way," he said. "Help me find my wife." He

waited for an answer, a voice from the heavens, a bolt of lightning, any kind of sign.

Nothing.

The drone of a city bus barreling up the street shattered the stillness of the moment. On its side was an enormous poster of Santa Claus ice-skating beneath the tree at Rockefeller Center, his back leg splayed out behind him.

Andrew felt a rush of hope. He knew where to find Beth.

CHAPTER EIGHTEEN

*T*he rink is now closed. Thank you all for coming, and have a merry Christmas."

Andrew heard the closing announcement crackle from the Rockefeller Center speakers as he jumped out of a cab at the corner of 5th and 47th and ran across the plaza to the skating rink.

Gripping the railing beneath the mighty tree, he scanned the rink below. The Christmas Eve crowd had dwindled to just a few dozen, and the last of the skaters were making their way off the ice as the Zamboni driver readied his big machine. For a moment, Andrew's heart sank. Could his hunch be wrong? What if she wasn't there?

Then a couple of teenage girls moved aside, and he could see Beth down by the rink. She was leaning against the railing, staring out at the ice, lost in thought. He watched her for a moment. She seemed so small and vulnerable, so alone.

"Not skating tonight?" Andrew sidled up beside his wife at the railing. Beth didn't look at him, didn't ask what he was doing there or how he'd known where to find her. She just ignored his question, kept staring straight ahead. Andrew hadn't taken the time to formulate his thoughts and had no earthly idea what came next. He took a breath, started again.

"Beth, I've loved you my whole life. Every memory that's ever meant anything to me had you in the starring role. And I would never deliberately do anything to hurt you."

Beth looked at him, and Andrew could tell by the pained look in her eyes that she wasn't convinced. He pressed on.

"I did a stupid thing and tried to convince myself that going to LA was the best thing for us. Of course, I should have talked it over with you. But I was arrogant and self-consumed, and all I could think about was money and success. I almost had myself convinced I was doing it for your own good. I was wrong, and I was foolish, but I'm not that guy anymore. I'm not that guy, and I will never be that guy again. Because I love you."

He turned her to him and took her face in his hands. He said it again this time while gazing right into her eyes. "I love *you*. I. Love. You."

Beth finally looked back at him. Her chin was quivering. "Beth, as long as I'm around, you will never be alone."

Hearing Andrew repeat the line he'd said to her on their wedding day seemed to break down Beth's last wall of resistance. The tears flowed—tears of relief, tears of desperation. Tears, he hoped, of forgiveness.

As the noisy Zamboni hummed its way across the ice, Andrew held his wife in his arms. She buried her face in his chest and cried as the snow started to fall harder and clung to their hair and shoulders. And when Andrew reached the point where he would usually break off the hug, he clung to her even tighter. He'd hold on forever if only he could, if only it meant his Beth would be there to hang on to.

Then an idea dawned on him, and he suddenly moved back. "I've got it!" he said. "I know what the gift is! You're going to skate!"

"What gift? Skate? Andrew, what are you talking about?"

Andrew grabbed her by the hand and pulled her with him. "Come on, you're skating! Don't you see! It's what you've always wanted! It's your secret wish!"

"Secret wish? But, Andrew, the rink's closed. It's too late."

Andrew grabbed a pair of skates from the rental rack, handed them to her. "It's never too late," he said. "Here. Put these on!"

"Andrew, no. We'll come back tomorrow."

"*No!* There is no tomorrow! Please, Beth. Just put them on. I'll be right back!"

Andrew vaulted over the railing and slipped and slid his way across the ice toward the Zamboni.

"Excuse me, sir! Could I speak with you for a moment?"

Andrew darted in front of the big machine to block its path, and the burly driver hit the brakes and yanked off his headphones. "Bub, you need to move off the ice. Rink's closed."

"I'm sorry, sir, but I can't do that. You see my wife over there?" Andrew gestured to Beth, who gave the man a little smile and wave. The driver instinctively waved back and then caught himself.

"This is her Christmas gift. Do you have a wife?" Andrew read the name sewn on the surly driver's shirt. "Dino?"

Dino glared at him. "Ex-wife."

"Great!" Andrew said. "Then you understand. You see, I forgot to get her a Christmas gift, and I'm really in hot water. She told me that if I could figure out a way for her to skate at Rockefeller Center, all by herself, then all would be forgiven. She doesn't think I can do it. Can you believe that? Kind of like the Giants last Sunday, eh? Down by four, with thirty-six seconds to play. Manning drops back, throws—touchdown! Can you help me get into the end zone, Dino?"

Dino the Zamboni driver scowled. Andrew figured he'd miscalculated. With his luck, the guy was probably a Jets fan.

"Please," Andrew said. "Just five minutes. I'll pay you." Andrew pulled out his wallet and started peeling off cash. "Here. You can have it all. There's a couple hundred bucks here."

Dino scowled down at him. "Keep your money. You got five minutes."

"Thank you, Dino! Thank you so much!"

Dino shifted the Zamboni into gear to move it off the ice. "Five minutes. Clock's running, buddy."

Watching from the railing, Andrew thought how beautiful and happy Beth looked as she cut slow circles across the lonely rink. She seemed to be swept up in the moment; her eyes were closed and a contented smile played on her lips.

Andrew heaved a sigh of relief. He could breathe again. He'd figured it out, solved the cosmic riddle. He'd found the one gift that would free him from fate's cruel spell. This was much more than a music box; this was a gift for the soul. Everything was going to be all right. The dreaded 11:58 would come and go, and Beth would be none the wiser. She wouldn't die tonight, or the next night, or for many years to come.

Little did Beth know that he'd given her more than a few minutes' skating time. He had given her back her future. Their future. Children. Grandchildren. Thousands of wonderful memories yet to make.

Andrew smiled as he watched her graceful glide. The lights from the mighty Christmas tree cast her in soft amber light, making her look almost like an—

"Angel."

Andrew turned to see that the Zamboni driver had silently eased up beside him at the railing. "She looks like an angel," Dino said.

Andrew nodded. "Yeah."

The burly driver was holding a cup of hot coffee. Andrew could see the logo on the side, a large golden key. He shook his head. "I guess you'd know all about angels. I never would have figured."

Dino chuckled. "Angels come in all shapes and sizes, you know."

"And apparently temperaments too," Andrew said.

Dino laughed out loud at this. "Nice you still got your sense of humor, Farmer. Considering you're almost out of time."

Andrew shot him a look. "Think again, bub. This is what she wanted. This is the gift."

Dino took a sip of coffee. "If only it were that easy."

Andrew squared off with him. "What do you mean? I got her the perfect gift. I did it! She knows how much I love her. I did everything I was asked!"

Dino looked at Beth gliding effortlessly across the ice. "This is a lovely gesture, but unfortunately, it's not the particular gift we were referring to."

"*Particular* gift?" Andrew said. "Now it's a *particular* gift? 'Put some thought into it,' you said. I did, and here we are. Exactly what Beth wanted. This is her dream, for crying out loud! You can't go changing the rules at the eleventh hour. I beat you!"

Dino found Andrew's outburst amusing. "Buddy, I'll tell you what—you got spunk." The angel gave Andrew a condescending pat on the back. "Give it some more thought. But don't think too long. The clock's ticking."

The big man winked at Andrew, then turned and walked away. Andrew could barely breathe.

A stone's throw away, the bells of St. Patrick's began to toll the hour of nine.

CHAPTER NINETEEN

*B*eth hooked her arm through Andrew's as they strolled the three blocks from the 86th Street subway station back to their Carnegie Hill apartment. She was beaming and still keyed up from her time on the ice.

"Thank you for my Christmas present," she said. "Thanks for making me skate."

Andrew stopped abruptly, turned her to him. "That wasn't your present," he said. "I'm going to get you another present. The real present. You just have to tell me what you want."

"Don't be silly. I don't want anything else."

"Sure you do. Think. I have to—I mean, I want to prove to you that I love you."

Beth shook her head. "Andrew, buying me something won't prove that you love me."

"Sure it will. I mean, it couldn't hurt, right? Just tell me. What is it you *really* want for Christmas? If you could have anything in the world."

"Well, I know a Christmas present we *both* got." Beth took his hands in hers. "I'm pregnant."

Andrew stared at her. The news was so sudden, so jolting and unexpected, that for a moment it didn't even register.

"What? When? How long have you known?" he said.

"About six weeks."

Andrew felt her watching him, searching his eyes for a sign, any kind of indication of how he felt about the sudden news.

"Sorry to just blurt it out like this on the street," she said. "But I kept waiting for the perfect moment to tell you, and now seems—well, as perfect as it's going to get."

Andrew felt frozen, hypnotized, as if he'd slipped into some carnival gypsy's trance. How could fate be so horribly void of compassion, so unthinkably cruel? When Beth was killed that night, she was keeping this secret. She had died carrying their child, and in a few short hours, unless he could figure out some way to stop it, she would die again. On this terrible night, he wasn't just losing his wife, his lifelong love and best friend. He was losing his child. Their child.

Beth's smile vanished. "This isn't exactly the reaction I was hoping for."

Then, at the moment when things could have gone from bad to irretrievably worse, Andrew Farmer made the save. He broke into a wide grin, clutched Beth in his arms, and pulled her to him.

"Oh, Beth! This is . . . the most amazingly perfect Christmas present ever!"

"Really, Andrew? You're really happy?"

Andrew's agent training was paying dividends. He could lie with the best of them. "Are you kidding?" he said. "There's nothing on earth I want more." Andrew took Beth's face in his hands and gave her a slow, sweet kiss. He whispered into her ear, "This is my dream."

"Can you believe it?" Beth said. "We're going to have a baby! We're going to be parents!" She wrapped her arms around his waist in a blissful embrace.

There on that cold, snowy Manhattan sidewalk on Christmas Eve, Andrew Farmer held his joyful wife and tried to navigate the swell of conflicting emotions swirling around in his head.

If only she knew.

If only she knew the dreadful secret he was keeping.

CHAPTER TWENTY

*C*areful. Watch the branches!"

Beth directed Andrew as he navigated their puny last-minute Christmas tree up the apartment stairwell. *Déjà vu,* he thought, careful not to crack the same branch he cracked the last time.

Beth fished the apartment key out of her coat pocket. "Can you believe they were still open?" she said. "Guess we aren't the only ones who wait till the last minute."

A branch poked Andrew in the cheek. "Ow! This tree doesn't like me much. That is, if you can call this oversized branch a tree."

"Hey!" Beth said. "I love Piney."

Andrew grinned. "Piney? You named this twig Piney?"

"Yes. He's family now."

Andrew placed the pathetic little tree in the same spot it sat the last time he lived the moment, then went to the CD player and popped in Beth's favorite Christmas album. The crooning voice of Andy Williams drifted through the apartment, and she smiled.

Together they trimmed the little tree, Beth singing along with the CD, lending her sweet voice to such classics as "White Christmas," "The Christmas Song," and "The First Noel."

Meanwhile, Andrew feigned calm as he struggled to control the knot of throbbing fear in his stomach. It was past ten o'clock. Less than two hours to go. He wondered how it would all play out and determined that he wouldn't go down without a battle. When the crucial moment came, he was going to make a stand. He was going to put up his dukes and fight back against Lady Fate or go down swinging.

He wondered if Lionel was watching him, if the angel could read his thoughts at that very moment. He glanced again at the clock: 10:39 p.m.

"There. Perfect," Beth said. She stepped back from the tree and smiled at their handiwork. "We don't want to overdecorate. Then it just gets gaudy."

"Gaudy," Andrew said. "Great word."

Beth kissed him on the cheek. "Hold on. There's one gift you get to open early." Beth went to the couch, reached underneath, and pulled out a thin gift-wrapped package.

"So that's where you hide them."

Beth handed him the present. "One of the places," she said. "Go ahead. Open it."

Andrew tore off the paper to reveal a book. He read the title out loud. "*She's Having a Baby—and I'm Having a Breakdown. What Every Man Needs to Know—and Do—When the Woman He Loves Is Pregnant.*" He smiled at Beth. "Perfect."

"I thought so," Beth said. "Oh, Andrew. I'm so excited! Just think, a year from tonight this apartment will be littered with toys!"

Andrew looked away. "Sounds wonderful," he said.

Beth moved in front of him and gave him an impish smile. "So, Mr. Farmer. Do you want to know? Do want to know if we're having a boy or a girl?"

Andrew brushed a stray hair back from her cheek and shook his head. "No."

"Me neither," Beth said. "One of life's great remaining mysteries." She kissed him and moved to the fireplace. "Picture it, Andrew. Next Christmas Eve there'll be three stockings on the mantel."

Andrew stepped over to her and wrapped his arms around her from behind. "There's nothing I want more," he said.

Beth turned to him. "You know what I want?" she said.

Andrew smiled as she led him by the hand back to the bedroom.

"Sooooo," Beth said with a twinkle. "Any name ideas yet?" They were curled up beneath the sheets in bed, her head on his chest. Andrew had one nervous eye on the digital clock on the bedside table. It was now 11:41 p.m. He felt a surge of hope. All he had to do was hold on to his wife for another seventeen minutes, and it would all be over. He would have managed to outmaneuver Providence. Life would go on. They'd have a future together, a family. And all this would seem like a bad dream.

"Andrew? Hello?" Beth gave him a playful pinch to see if he was awake.

"Oh, well, I don't know. Whatever name you want," Andrew said.

"No!" Beth said. "We have to decide together. I want to do everything together. We're a team, right?"

"Right. Beth, is that clock accurate?"

Beth looked from the clock to her anxious husband. "Why the clock watching? Am I boring you?"

"Of course not. I just want to make sure we don't miss Christmas."

"Miss Christmas? Andrew, what are you talking about?"

"Nothing, it's just—never mind."

Beth smiled at him. "Don't take this the wrong way . . ."

"Uh-oh," Andrew said. "Nothing good ever starts with 'Don't take this the wrong way.'"

Beth smacked him on the arm. "Oh, stop it! I just wanted to thank you for helping me realize something about myself."

"Oh?" Andrew said. "What?"

"Well, when we first moved to New York, I was totally dependent on you. I thought that without you I wouldn't be able to survive. I used to cry when you left the apartment in the morning. I missed River Falls so much."

"Really?"

"Uh-huh. But now I know that coming to New York changed my life in a way I never could have imagined. A good way. I found myself here, my identity. I started my own business, made my own way. I grew up."

Andrew stroked her hair. "I know," he said. "And I'm so proud of you."

Beth snuggled close and breathed a contented sigh. "I love you, Andrew."

"I love you too." He softly caressed her hair and watched the clock switch to 11:46.

Twelve minutes to go. He thought about Lionel. Maybe he'd given up. Maybe he'd decided that Andrew had done enough, been through enough. Maybe he was needed elsewhere, assigned to some other poor sap at the other end of the universe. Andrew looked down at his wife. Her eyes were closed, her breathing restful. Asleep. He allowed himself a smile. It was all over but the touchdown dance. Everything was going to be all right.

She rolled over, popped open one eye. "I'm starving," she said. She started to roll out of bed, but Andrew jumped up.

"No!" he said. "Stay in bed. I'll get you something."

Beth frowned at him. "Are you okay?"

"Yes! I just— you stay here. Rest. I'll go find something."

"It's okay, honey." Before Andrew could protest, Beth was up and reaching for her robe. "I'd rather look for myself."

"Beth, please. I can make a list of what we have and read it to you."

Beth laughed. "Honey, the baby's still a long way off. I don't need to take it that easy, not just yet." She threw on her robe. "Besides, you don't know where anything is. Relax. I'll be right back."

Andrew grabbed his jeans from the floor. "I'll go with you."

Beth held up a hand. "Andrew, chill. I'm just going to the

refrigerator." She left the room and Andrew sat back down on the edge of the bed, tried taking a few calming breaths and again looked at the bedside clock: 11:48. *It's okay*, he told himself. *We're almost there. Just ten more minutes.*

Beth called from the kitchen, "Hey, how about some ice cream?"

Andrew called back, "No, thank you." As nervous as he was, he knew he couldn't hold down so much as a cracker. "Just come back in here."

"Yeah, it's too cold for ice cream," Beth said. "How about a bagel?"

"No. I'm fine. Beth, please come back to bed."

He could hear Beth continue her rummaging.

"Or we have this weirdly shaped fruitcake from Aunt Vera in Boca Raton," she said. "Eww. Maybe not. I think it might be alive."

"I'm not hungry, Beth. I'd really like it if you just came back to—"

The phone rang.

"I'll get it!" Andrew shouted loudly enough to be heard in the next building. He jumped up from the bed and started yanking back blankets looking for the phone. It rang again. "Where is that stupid phone?" he said.

"Hello?" He heard Beth pick up in the kitchen and froze. He listened intently, one eye on the clock: 11:49. He could tell from Beth's tone that she knew the caller.

"Of course," she said. "Don't worry about it. I'm on the case." Andrew heard the sound of the phone being plopped back on the counter.

A moment later Beth breezed back into the bedroom and made a beeline for the walk-in closet. "Minor crisis," she said. She hurriedly slipped on a pair of jeans and a pullover sweater. "That was Mrs. Applebee. Lulu got out again."

"I'll go." Andrew started frantically yanking on his pants.

"Honey, it's fine," Beth said. "She never gets far. I'll just be a minute."

"No, you can't—" Andrew's pants bunched up; he lost his balance and fell to the floor. Beth laughed; he was sure he looked ridiculous as he struggled to his feet. "Let *her* look!" he said. "It's her dog. She should be more careful."

Beth chuckled. "Be more careful? Andrew, she's over ninety years old."

"The fresh air will be good for her circulation," Andrew said. He was finally able to stand up and get his pants on, then began a frantic search for his shirt, lost somewhere in the blankets.

Beth laughed as she zipped up her jeans and slipped into a pair of tennis shoes. "Andrew, go back to bed. I'll just be a minute."

"Nope. I'm going with you."

Andrew finally found his T-shirt. As Beth headed out of the room, he stumbled after her, hopping on one foot as he tried to walk and put on shoes at the same time.

By the time he was able to actually accomplish this, Beth was at the front door putting on her woolen jacket and scarf.

"I'll do it," Andrew said.

"Andrew, you know Lulu hates you," Beth said. "All dogs do."

"What? No, he doesn't!"

"He's a *she*," Beth said. "She won't come to you. You'll spook her."

"Then I'll just come along for support. I feel like a walk."

Beth shook her head. "What is with you tonight? Too much eggnog?" She gave him a quick peck on the cheek. "Be right back."

Andrew caught a quick glimpse of the grandfather clock behind her: 11:52. Beth buttoned up her coat. "No, Beth. Please don't go. It's not your problem."

"Baby, the poor woman's worried," Beth said. She slipped on her gloves. "And it's Christmas Eve."

"Exactly," Andrew said. "The nerve, asking you to go out this late on Christmas Eve. It's almost 11:58."

Beth gave him a curious smile. "Huh?"

"I mean, midnight. It's almost midnight."

Beth stepped up to him and took his face in her gloved hands. "It seems the baby news has made you a little loopy. You act as if you're never going to see me again."

Andrew looked away. He couldn't meet her eyes. "Beth, please don't . . ."

Andrew stopped. Over Beth's shoulder he saw Lionel, standing on the other side of the door, his stern eyes locked on him.

"You can't change this, Andrew. This is her destiny." The angel's words were firm and strong. He meant business.

"No!" Andrew shouted.

Beth shook her head. "You are being so weird." She gave him a quick kiss on the lips. "Weird, but adorable."

"It's her time, Andrew," Lionel said.

"It's not fair," Andrew said. He was trembling, his knees quaking, his heart beating as if it might burst.

Beth winked at him. "Life's not fair," she said. "Keep my spot warm."

Andrew felt her move away from him, and every fiber of his being screamed, *Grab her! Hold on for dear life! Do something, anything, to keep her from walking out that door.*

But he was paralyzed. He simply couldn't will himself to move. His eyes locked on Lionel's.

"No," he whispered.

Then she was gone, out the door into the freezing Christmas Eve night to keep her date with destiny. The dreadful sound of the door closing snapped Andrew out of his trance.

He lunged for the door, grabbed the knob, and pulled. It wouldn't open. He pointed at Lionel. "Open it! If you're truly from God, open it! I order you to open this door!"

"I don't work for you, Andrew."

"Please! I beg you—"

"You know the rules, Andrew. You got your three days, and now we get Beth. It'd be so much easier on you if you'd just accept that."

"I'll never accept it! Never!"

"Give it up, Farmer. It's over."

This calm pronouncement of finality sent a shot of grief through Andrew that overwhelmed him. He began to sob uncontrollably. His knees abandoned him, and he slumped to the floor. Anguished tears rolled out of him. He buried his face in his hands and cried like a lost little boy.

"Please. Please, Lionel. I'll give anything."

"*Anything?*" Lionel said.

Andrew slowly looked up into Lionel's eyes. Did he detect a flicker of hope in the angel's tone? Andrew rose to his feet and wiped his face with his sleeve. "Yes," he said. *"Anything."*

And suddenly the truth hit Andrew Farmer like a runaway train. The *gift.* The one gift his wife really needed for Christmas. Not a music box or a turn on the ice. A chance. A chance only he could offer her.

At last, Andrew knew what he had to do. He knew what he must give.

As the realization washed over him, Andrew nodded, and a small smile creased Lionel's wise and ageless face. The grandfather clock by the door read 11:55.

Their eyes met. Human and angel. The door lock turned, the door swung open, and Andrew Farmer ran out after his wife.

CHAPTER TWENTY-ONE

*T*he snow clung like a thin cotton blanket to the sidewalks and pavement of New York City. Andrew ran madly down the middle of the nearly empty street, a determined man with a desperate purpose and not a moment to spare.

He turned a corner, slipped, and hit the ground hard. As he sprang back up, headlights and the grill of a blaring city bus bore down on him. He jumped out of the way, kept moving, moving forward toward Third Avenue, where fate awaited him.

As Beth reached the corner at 88th and Third, she heard Lulu's familiar yelp. She stopped and looked around. It wouldn't be easy to spot a white dog in a snowstorm. Then she saw the trembling little terrier parked in the middle of the street. Beth breathed a sigh of relief and gave a quick prayer of thanks for the fact that there was scarcely a car in sight to threaten the little pup on this stormy Christmas Eve.

"Lulu?" The dog's tail wagged at Beth's familiar voice. "Hey, you crazy girl. What are you doing out here?"

Andrew rounded the corner at a dead run just as Beth crouched down in front of the dog. He watched Beth scoop the pup up in her arms. The sound of the speeding cab seemed louder than before, so deafening it nearly drowned him out.

"Beth!"

He did the math as he dashed for his wife. He had the angle on the taxi, but the car was moving so much faster. There was no way he could make it. It was too late. He had no chance. He could see Beth as she turned toward the sound of the screaming engine. She was bathed in headlights, and he could see her watching the speeding taxi as it bore down on her, kicking up a dusty white wake as it zoomed toward its deadly destiny.

As he sprinted toward her, time seemed to slow down, and Andrew saw it all happening again. He was a hundred feet from her, then fifty. He felt his hamstring pull and pushed even harder. This time he wouldn't be a helpless spectator; this time he wouldn't be too late.

He saw Beth stare at the fast-moving death machine with unblinking eyes, as if she couldn't quite believe what was happening.

In the moment before impact, Beth performed one final unselfish act. She tossed the skittish dog out of the way. Again, the cabbie saw her much too late, tires skidding on the icy street. There was no way to brake, no time to swerve.

For a flickering moment, Beth watched her life flash before her. The end had come far too soon for the young mom-to-be and her unborn child.

I am going to die, she thought. *My life is over.*

Suddenly, Beth felt herself being lifted off the ground. Only it was not the crushing metal of the taxi's front bumper that had hit her. It was Andrew who slammed into her like a charging linebacker. He knocked her out of the street and into a big pile of plastic garbage bags that cushioned her landing.

Beth watched as Andrew stood in her place and defiantly faced the skidding taxi. He didn't flinch or cower. He just stood there staring right into the headlights.

"Nooo!" Beth screamed as the taxi slammed into her husband, knocking him fifty feet back down the street. The impact was horrific and devastating and final.

In the moments before his death, Andrew Farmer was strangely calm. He'd been given three days to find a way to save Beth's life, and he'd accomplished the task just in the nick of time.

Andrew had always wondered if he'd have the courage to give his life for someone he loved. And now, in the last instant of his life, he had his answer. He would die knowing that he had what it took, that he was willing to make the ultimate sacrifice. His wife, his beloved friend, his Beth, would be all right. She would have their baby and be a wonderful mother and move on.

He had done it. He had given Beth the greatest Christmas gift possible.

He had given her his life.

"Andrew!"

Beth's initial shock turned into a desperate scream. As she rushed to her fallen husband, Beth knew in her heart there wouldn't be a happy ending this Christmas. She knew that Andrew Farmer, the love of her life, the father of her unborn child, wasn't going to make it.

CHAPTER TWENTY-TWO

*M*rs. Farmer?" The ER doctor came through the door into the waiting area, and Beth lunged to her feet. She had been waiting for nearly an hour with no word, and she felt that if she had to wait another minute she would go stark raving mad.

"I'm Dr. Atkinson, and I'm afraid—" The kindly doctor took a deep breath and shook her head. Beth felt her heart sink.

"I'm so sorry," the doctor said. "We did everything we could."

"No," Beth said. "There must be something more you can do." The tears rolled down Beth's face and into the corners of her mouth.

"I think you should say your good-byes," the doctor said. Beth wiped the tears from her face with the sleeve of her sweater and followed the doctor down a long white corridor.

Moments later, Beth stood in the doorway of a dim, dreary trauma room. There was only one soft light and the faint green glow of the heart monitor to illuminate it. Andrew Farmer lay motionless on the examining table, a white sheet covering everything but his head.

From where she was standing, Beth thought how pale and small he looked. She hesitated; she was afraid to approach him, for she wasn't sure her legs would hold her up even for the few short steps to the table. She glanced over at the barely beeping heart monitor and then moved toward her lifeless husband.

Standing over Andrew, Beth gently fingered the bandage that was wrapped around the top of his head. His eyes were black and sunken as if he'd gotten the worst end of some back-alley brawl.

She reached down, took his lifeless hand, and held it to her quivering lips. "What were you thinking? Shoving me out of the way like that. It should have been me. It should have been—"

The heart monitor stuttered, flat-lined, and let out a monotonous, piercing wail. Startled, Beth dropped Andrew's hand as if she were the cause of it.

"Andrew, no! Andrew!"

The doors flew open, and Dr. Atkinson rushed in. She checked Andrew's heart with her stethoscope, then switched off the sound on the monitor and put a hand on Beth's arm.

"I'm truly sorry for your loss, Mrs. Farmer."

When the doctor retreated from the room, the last thread of Beth's composure snapped. She began to sob uncontrollably. She put her head on Andrew's chest and desperately listened for the heartbeat that was no longer there.

"Andrew, I love you. I love you so much . . . I'll always love you."

Her faltering words were finally drowned out in sobs. He was gone now. Her best friend had left her behind to raise their child alone.

Beth almost didn't see it when it came. One faint pulse of the flat green line against its black background. Then another. She stood up and peered at the heart monitor. Did she imagine it? Then it came again . . . another pulse . . . and another. She stared hard at the green line. The flat line shot upward again and again. The heart rate counter rose from zero to ten beats a minute, then twenty, then thirty.

"Andrew?"

Andrew opened his bruised eyes a slit and looked up at his wife.

"Oh, Andrew! You're alive! You've come back to me!"

Beth took Andrew's face in her hands and kissed him. "I thought I'd lost you," she said. "Do you know what it feels like to lose the love of your life?"

"I can imagine," Andrew said. "I can imagine."

EPILOGUE

*B*eth wasn't entirely right. There weren't three stockings on the mantel the next Christmas. There were four.

Henry Farmer's stocking hung right next to his baby grandson Lionel's. The old man who thought he was living his final chapter at a nursing home found he actually had a few more left in him. Baby Lionel gave him a new reason to live. So Grandpa Henry moved in with his son and daughter-in-law to watch the little guy grow up firsthand.

Now, don't think Andrew and Beth Farmer have a perfect life. We don't. But there's one thing for certain: we love each other deeply, and those three days changed me in ways I never thought possible. I learned to be grateful for the good in this life, to appreciate the little things and the insignificant moments. To treat every single day as if it were my last.

If you have a grateful heart, then no matter what the number on your bank balance reads, you're as wealthy as the richest tycoon.

And it's forever Christmas.

READING GROUP GUIDE

1. Andrew admitted in the prologue that ingratitude was his defining characteristic. What do you think he meant by this? Is being grateful really important to a happy and successful life? How did Andrew's lack of gratitude contribute to the story?

2. Childhood sweethearts Andrew and Beth have drifted apart. What do think caused this? In general, what causes married couples to grow apart? What qualities in a marriage partner help keep a marriage going strong?

3. Andrew's obsession with material success causes him to lose sight of what's really important. Why doesn't he value Beth's career choice? How did Andrew's and Beth's views of success differ? Is there a higher, more spiritual meaning of success than the commonly held materialistic view?

4. How do you think Andrew's lack of a strong father figure affected his own desire to be a father? How did his anger towards his father influence and affect his life and marriage?

5. When Andrew's mother passed away, he deeply resented his father for not being there: so much so he tried to convince Beth to share in his hate for his dad. How does Beth react to this? What does her refusal to participate in his hatred say about her character? What other moments in the novel give insight into Beth's character?

6. Despite his love for his wife, Andrew takes Beth for granted. Have you ever taken someone you love for granted? Do you feel that, perhaps, you've been taken for granted?

7. Andrew is doubly devastated by Beth's death because she died thinking he'd been unfaithful to her. Have you ever experienced regret over how you treated someone? Why is reconciliation important? How is reconciliation a part of this story?

8. How might the story have gone differently if Andrew had actually cheated with Kimberly? How would you have felt about his character if he had done this? Would he still have been able to redeem himself in your eyes?

9. When Andrew initially encounters Lionel, he doesn't at first recognize him as a heavenly visitant. Why do we sometimes fail to distinguish God's voice? What state of thought sometimes blocks our receptivity to God's word? What do you think Lionel's key symbolizes?

10. If you had three days to live how would you spend them? If you were Andrew and knew Beth was about to die, would you tell her? How do think things might have gone differently if he had told her?

11. Do you agree with Beth's decision to keep her friendship

with Andrew's estranged father a secret? How did this revelation in River Falls contribute to the conflict of the story? Why was it important that Andrew miss the train from River Falls to New York?

12. How does Andrew's concept of the "gift" evolve throughout the story? What's the difference between the first gift he gave Beth and the ultimate gift?

13. Andrew encounters a variety of "angels" during the three days. What do you think their purpose was in Andrew's experience? What forms might angels appear in our own lives?

14. When Andrew's desperately searching for Beth around their Manhattan neighborhood, he pauses to pray, asks God to help him find his way. He expected his answer to come as "a voice from heaven, a bolt of lightning, any kind of sign." Instead, a bus rolled by with a Rockefeller Center advertisement that sparked his memory. Have you ever tried to outline how God should speak to you? Have you ever had a prayer answered in an unexpected way?

15. Why do people sometimes have to hit rock bottom before they are ready to make a change? What does Andrew's final sacrifice say about how his heart changed from the beginning of the book to the end? Is there anyone you would give your life for?

16. By the end of the book, Andrew learns an important lesson about gratitude? What do you think he learned? Why is it important to be grateful for the good in our lives?

ACKNOWLEDGMENTS

*T*his book is about gratitude: gratitude for friendship, for love, for all the good that God gives us, the sweet companionships that nurture our heart and soul and richly bless our lives.

As a core theme of this novel is gratitude, I'd be remiss if I didn't express a little of my own for the many extraordinary and talented people who took the reins of this project and helped guide it to completion.

I'll begin with my tireless agents Jennifer Gates and Natasha Alexis of the Zachary Shuster Harmsworth Agency. Thank you, Jen and Natasha, for being willing to take a chance on me. Your insight, brilliant notes, and encouragement made all the difference.

I'll be forever grateful to Penny Stokes, an editor extraordinaire with a quick pen, a brilliant mind, and a kind heart. Thank you, Penny, from the bottom of *my* heart for all you did to make this book better.

Thomas Nelson truly is a writer's dream. There are so many good people there who obviously love their jobs and whose talents are helping to bring about literary works that have blessed and will continue to bless the world. I'm especially grateful for my editor, Becky Monds. Becky, thank you for believing in this project and for being such a calm and steady presence along the way.

I'd like to also express gratitude for the rest of the Thomas Nelson-Zondervan Fiction staff for working so diligently to bring this book to fruition. Thank you Ansley Boatman, Katie Bond, Amanda Bostic, Karli Cajka, Laura Dickerson, Elizabeth Hudson, Jodi Hughes, Ami McConnell, Becky Philpott, and Kerri Potts. A special thanks goes to Vice President and Publisher Daisy Hutton for leading such an extraordinary team!

The support of family and friends is so important to whatever we accomplish in life. I'm grateful to my wonderfully supportive wife, Gina, and my beautiful and talented daughter Chloe June. Thanks to all the remarkable people who have populated my life thus far. By your love and friendship, you've made the journey such a rich and rewarding experience.

Lastly, and most importantly, I must express my gratitude and love to God for guiding me every step of the way. That wonderfully simple statement in the book of John pretty much sums it up. *"I can of mine own self do nothing."*

ABOUT THE AUTHOR

Photo by Bob Lovett

Robert Tate Miller began his writing career with homespun essays of small-town life that were published by *Reader's Digest*, *The Christian Science Monitor*, and the Chicken Soup for the Soul book series. He moved to Los Angeles in the late 1980s and wrote successful family-oriented telefilms for NBC, ABC Family, and the Hallmark Channel. Robert lives in Northridge, California, with his wife, Gina, and stepdaughter, Chloe June.

Facebook: RobertTateMiller

Twitter @Robtatemiller